Ra
the
Mighty

THE GREAT
TOMB ROBBERY

Ra
the
Mighty

THE GREAT
TOMB ROBBERY

BY

A. B. Greenfield

ILLUSTRATED BY

Sarah Horne

HOLIDAY HOUSE · New York

Text copyright © 2019 by Amy Butler Greenfield
Illustrations copyright © 2019 by Sarah Horne
All Rights Reserved
HOLIDAY HOUSE is registered in the U.S. Patent and Trademark Office.
Printed and bound in May 2019 at Maple Press, York, PA, USA.
The artwork was created with pen and ink with a digital finish.
www.holidayhouse.com
First Edition
1 3 5 7 9 10 8 6 4 2

Library of Congress Cataloging-in-Publication Data
Names: Greenfield, Amy Butler, 1968- author. | Horne, Sarah, 1979-
illustrator.
Title: Ra the mighty : the great tomb robbery / by A. B. Greenfield ;
illustrated by Sarah Horne.
Other titles: Great tomb robbery
Description: First edition. | New York : Holiday House, [2019] | Summary: The
pharaoh's pampered cat Ra and his scarab beetle sidekick solve the mystery
of a ransacked tomb in ancient Egypt. | Includes bibliographical
references.
Identifiers: LCCN 2018060592 | ISBN 9780823442409 (hardcover)
Subjects: | CYAC: Cats—Fiction. | Scarabs—Fiction. | Animals—Fiction. |
Tombs—Fiction. | Robbers and outlaws—Fiction. | Egypt—History—To 332
B.C.—Fiction. | Mystery and detective stories.
Classification: LCC PZ7.G8445 Rd 2019 | DDC [Fic]—dc23
LC record available at https://lccn.loc.gov/2018060592

For Vivian, Carlo, and Sofia,
wonderful readers, travelers,
and cousins —A. B. G.

CHAPTER 1

Pampering

I'm not hard to please. Ask anyone. But when you're covered with fur and you've spent two full days traveling up the Nile under the fiery summer sun, you expect a little pampering. Especially if you're Ra the Mighty, Pharaoh's Cat.

Luckily, I travel with my own special pampering crew. We reached the palace at Thebes at dawn, and they whisked me away to Pharaoh's private garden. There they offered me a cushion and a snack of spiced ibex while they unpacked their brushes and perfumes.

I was on my third chunk of ibex when a tiny voice piped up from somewhere between my ears. "Ra? You're not really

going to wear perfume, are you?"

"Of course I am," I said. "I know you haven't been to Thebes before, but it's a noble city with high standards. Trust me, it's a glamorous place. I always wear perfume here."

"Then I'm getting off." My fur rippled, and my buddy Khepri bounded onto the stones by my cushion. For a scarab beetle, he's pretty quick on his feet. It must be all that dung-rolling he does.

"Suit yourself." I snarfed up the last chunk of ibex. "But if you ask me, a little perfume wouldn't hurt you, Khepri. Anyone who spends as much time with dung as you do—"

"Dung smells *wonderful*," Khepri protested.

"I beg to differ." I rolled onto my side as the attendants came forward with their brushes. "You won't catch me smelling like a dung pile, ever."

Not for the first time, I was glad my attendants couldn't understand a word Khepri and I were saying. (Humans never do.)

"You're missing out, Ra," Khepri said earnestly.

"I'm not missing a thing," I said. "Jasmine, lily, myrrh—that's what I call perfume."

"Blech." Khepri backed up until he was a safe distance away from the perfume bottles. "I think I'll go explore the palace."

"Sure," I said, yawning. I bent my head

and allowed the attendants to smooth the fur between my ears. (That's the bit Khepri always rucks up.) "You go on ahead. I'll catch up with you later."

"Great," Khepri chirped. "By then, maybe I'll have a new case for us."

I lifted my head. "Oh, Khepri. Not that again." We had solved exactly one mystery together, and I had thought that was plenty. But Khepri had other ideas.

"You need to be more open, Ra," Khepri insisted. "I keep bringing you cases, and you keep turning them down. The case of the missing loaves—"

"They weren't missing," I said. "The baker's assistant miscounted. He's never been good with numbers."

"—and the case of the mysterious stranger—"

"I told you: it was the Assyrian ambassador."

"—and the case of the disappearing dung pile—"

"Khepri, I draw the line at dung." I twisted so that the attendants could brush my tummy. "We're Great Detectives, my friend. We require a Great Mystery, not some piddling little nothing of a case. When a Great Mystery appears, then I'll get involved. But not before."

"Well, I'd be okay with a Small Mystery," Khepri said. "Even a Very Small Mystery."

"You're right, Khepri," said a brisk voice behind us. "Even a Very Small Mystery would be good for Ra."

It was our fellow Great Detective, Miu—kitchen cat extraordinaire. I flipped over and braced myself. Miu is a terrific friend, brave and loyal, but she has this strange idea that the life I lead doesn't build character. (Honestly! Everyone knows that Pharaoh's Cat is born with oodles of character. He hardly needs more.)

I greeted her with a ripple of my whiskers. "I thought you were going to stay on the boat and search for stowaway rats."

"Job done," Miu reported with pride. She rubbed a paw over her torn ear, clearing a cobweb away. "How about you, Ra? Have you accomplished anything since we arrived?"

"I've accomplished a snack," I said.

Miu's whiskers twitched. "That doesn't count."

"Sure it counts." I yawned and went floppy again. The attendants were getting to my tail—my favorite bit.

"No matter how many times I see this, I can't believe it," Miu said, watching. "Cats are supposed to clean themselves, Ra. Like this." She started licking her hindquarters.

I shut my eyes. "Uggh. I'm willing to give myself a quick touch-up here and there. But a serious cleaning? Licking dirt off with my *tongue*? You've got to be kidding me."

"We're cats," Miu said. "That's what we do."

"Not Pharaoh's Cat," I insisted. "I have people for that. See?" The attendants gave me one last stroke, then picked up their perfume bottles.

"Perfume?" Miu looked scandalized. "Ra, that's a step too far."

"This is Thebes, Miu. You haven't really seen the place yet, but that's how they do things around here." As the attendants rubbed their perfumes into my fur, I sniffed at the air with a glad sigh. "Mmmm . . . this

is my favorite. Jasmine with overtones of lotus."

Miu wrinkled her nose. "Somebody needs to save you from yourself, Ra."

I waved a languid paw. "I'm fine. No saving needed."

Miu ignored me. She's a very strong-minded cat. "Khepri, we're going to have to intervene. We need to find a mystery for Ra, and fast."

Khepri clicked his forelegs in agreement. "Aye, aye!"

I had other ideas. Duty done, the attendants bowed and stepped back. I rose from my cushion, gave myself a good stretch, then strutted toward the door.

"Ra, where are you going?" Miu asked.

Khepri scuttled after me. "Yes, where?"

I paused at the doorway. "It's a mystery," I told them, and bounded away.

CHAPTER 2

Great Pharaoh's Cat

Pampered or not, I can move fast when I want to. By the time Miu and Khepri caught up with me, I'd reached my destination: the side courtyard.

Khepri hopped off Miu and clambered onto me. "What's going on, Ra?"

"Tell you in a minute," I said.

Pharaoh stood with his guards arrayed around him. His gold-embroidered tunic shone in the sun. Before him, bowing low, was the Vizier of the South, the top official in Thebes. As Pharaoh's deputy, he was responsible for managing the palace, collecting taxes, and enforcing the law in his domain.

Seeing me, Pharaoh broke off his conversation with the Vizier. "Ra, you look

The VIZIER

magnificent. Vizier, you remember my cat?"

"Indeed I do." Turning toward me, the Vizier bowed still more deeply. "Ra the Mighty, Lord of the Powerful Paw, Great Pharaoh's Cat, how very good to welcome you again to the royal palace at Thebes."

The bow was a nice touch, but I wasn't fooled. The Vizier had never been a fan of mine, not since the day I attacked his wig and chewed it up in front of the whole court. (It looked like a rat, I swear.) I was only a frisky kitten then, so you'd think he'd forgive and forget. But he hasn't.

When Pharaoh wasn't looking, the Vizier curled his lip at me. I curled mine right back, showing my pointy teeth.

Pharaoh smiled down on us both. "We are glad you're pleased to see Ra, Vizier. Especially as you'll be spending the whole day together."

The Vizier choked. "The wh-whole day? O Ruler of Rulers, I am not worthy."

"Possibly not," Pharaoh agreed, "but we need you to bring Ra to the Valley of the Kings today. He is to pose for the artists who are working on our tomb. They will create a wall painting of him and a sculpture, both as large as life."

"There," I said to Miu and Khepri. "Now you see why I wanted a proper brushing."

Miu looked confused. "You're wearing perfume for your *tomb*?"

"It's all part of the package," I told her. "It sets a distinctive tone."

She rubbed a paw against her nose. "It certainly does."

"I've always wanted to see the Valley of the Kings," Khepri said wistfully, high on the top of my head. "That's where the pharaohs are buried in their pyramids, right?"

"You need to keep up with the times," I told him. "Nobody builds pyramids anymore, Khepri. Too old-fashioned. Too obvious. Might as well put up a huge sign saying 'Robbers, here's the treasure.' That's why the pharaohs switched to the Valley of the Kings. It's guarded, it's private, and it's only for royals. They build the tombs into the cliffs, and once they're sealed, most people can't even guess where the entrances are."

"So there's nothing to see?" Khepri sounded disappointed.

"Oh, there's plenty of desert cliffs, if you like that sort of thing. They're quite majestic, if you catch them in the right light. And you could probably peek in at Pharaoh's tomb-in-progress—"

"Ooooh." Khepri perked up. "Really?"

"I don't see why not. And while you're there, we can look at mine, too. I can't remember what I've told you about it—"

"Pharaoh designed it," Khepri chirped.

"It's going to have a chamber connected to his," Miu put in.

"And walls patterned in carnelian and lapis lazuli—"

"And paintings of your favorite pool—"

"And a gilded cat bed—"

"With a jeweled cushion—"

"And little clay servants—"

"To brush your fur—"

"And a cat-shaped sarcophagus," Khepri finished.

"Do I really talk about it so much?" I said.

"Oh, no," said Khepri.

"Oh, yes," said Miu.

"Well, who can blame me?" I said happily. "It's going to be quite extraordinary. And did I mention the snacks?" Merely thinking about them made me lick my lips: wooden boxes packed to the brim with mummified quail and ibex and mutton and antelope. "I won't go hungry in the afterlife, that's for sure."

As far as I'm concerned, that's the whole point of a tomb. A gilded cat bed and a jeweled cushion are nice accessories, and I'm fond of the clay servants that will wait on me for all eternity, but it's the food I care about most—and not just because I'm a bit of a gourmet. The priests say you need two things for a good afterlife: a properly preserved mummy, and enough food to sustain your spirit. If you don't have those, then you can kiss the hereafter good-bye.

"Of course, everything's a work in progress at the moment," I reminded Miu and Khepri. "That's why I need to go pose."

Khepri was practically bouncing between my ears. "Ra, can I come with you?"

"Sure," I said. "You can entertain me while they draw. You come too, Miu."

She scratched her side with her hind paw. "I'll pass."

"How can you say no, Miu?" Chittering with excitement, Khepri danced by my ear. "A whole day in the Valley of the Kings—wow! We can go exploring, Ra. And maybe we'll find a Great Mystery. Something spooky, maybe—or even buried treasure."

"Sorry, Khepri. I'll be too busy posing." He looked so disappointed that I added, "But you can look around by yourself if you want to."

Khepri looked down at his tiny forelegs. "I won't get very far on my own."

I couldn't deny it. Scarabs are small, and the Valley of the Kings is vast.

Miu sighed. "Never mind, Khepri. If you want to go exploring, I'll take you."

Khepri looked up. "But you said you weren't coming."

Miu regarded him fondly. "I changed my mind."

A few feet away, Pharaoh was wrapping things up with the Vizier. "One last point, Vizier: we have heard rumors of discontent among the tomb workers."

The Vizier still had his head down. "O Ruler of Rulers, do not for one moment trouble yourself. The tomb workers are delighted to serve you, as are we all. We are not worthy even to look upon your feet—"

"Vizier, you will find out what the trouble is and report back to us before the end of the day." Pharaoh spoke in his no-nonsense voice—a voice I knew all too well from my early clawing-the-furniture days.

The Vizier was no fool. "O Ruler of Rulers, I shall go this very minute."

"Indeed you shall." Pharaoh gestured toward the back of the courtyard. Six men came forward, bearing a fancy litter (or people carrier, as I sometimes call it). Backing away from Pharaoh with a series of half-bows, the Vizier crawled under its fine linen canopy.

"Up you go, Ra," Pharaoh said.

"Hang on," I whispered to Khepri. Leaping onto the litter, I landed almost in the Vizier's lap—a serious miscalculation on my part. The Vizier's hand clamped down on the scruff of my neck. With the canopy hiding his grip from Pharaoh, he tried to shove me off the litter.

Khepri darted out of my fur and ran across the Vizier's hand. The Vizier yelped and released me. "Nice work," I murmured as Khepri hopped back onto my head.

"A beetle!" The Vizier's lips twisted in disgust. "Crawling in the cat's fur . . ."

Honestly, humans get so worked up about bugs.

"It's a scarab," Pharaoh explained. "The sacred creature is often with Ra these days. It's a great mark of divine favor."

"Did you hear that, Ra?" a tiny voice called out from between my ears. "I'm a mark of divine favor."

"You don't say?" I sampled a morsel of the roast mutton Pharaoh's servants had kindly provided. "And here I thought you were simply my buddy."

"Just what I need," the Vizier muttered under his breath. "A spoiled cat with a dung beetle on his head."

He was bent so low that he must have thought no one could hear him. But

Pharaoh's face darkened. "What did you say, Vizier?"

The Vizier glanced up in alarm and offered Pharaoh a weak smile. "O Ruler of Rulers, I said . . . er . . . it's just what I need—a royal cat with a sacred beetle on his head." He patted me, avoiding the spot that Khepri occupied. "What could be a better omen for the day?"

"Indeed." Pharaoh regarded me with affection. "Ra is the ideal traveling companion. May Amon-Ra guard you both on your journey."

Giving me a last wave, he turned away. The six bearers hoisted the litter to shoulder height.

"Where's Miu?" Khepri whispered anxiously.

A mottled ball of fur vaulted into the litter. "Sorry," Miu said. "I had to chase down a rat."

The Vizier looked in disgust at Miu. "I suppose you're under royal protection, too." Glancing out at Pharaoh's retreating back, he nudged us all away from him. "If I see so much as a single cat hair on my robes, you'll all pay the price. And I'm not going to even mention the word *dung*."

You just did, I thought, and I knew Khepri was thinking the same thing, because he giggled.

I stretched out comfortably at the front of the litter and started shredding the Vizier's pillows. Miu settled down beside me.

The Vizier huffed and looked the other way.

The litter swayed, and Khepri clicked his forelegs in delight. "We're off to the Valley of the Kings!"

CHAPTER 3

The Place of Truth

The sun was hot. The litter was comfy. As we crossed the Nile and journeyed into the desert, I finished the snacks and fell asleep, dreaming of stewed antelope and roast quail.

"Wake up, Ra!" Khepri blared in my ear.

I kept my eyes closed and tried to push him away with my paw. "Khepri, please!" *One more bite of antelope . . .*

"Ra, we're here," Miu said. "At least, I think we are."

I opened my eyes—and wished I hadn't. The walled, mud-brick village before me looked as dry and dusty as the cliffs behind it, a far cry from the elegance of Thebes. But I recognized the place. I'd made the trip here a few years ago, when Pharaoh selected our tomb site.

"It's Set Ma'at," I told Khepri and Miu. "The Place of Truth."

Khepri looked confused. "I thought we were going to the Valley of the Kings."

"The Valley starts there." I bobbed my head to indicate the high cliffs just north of us. "But Set Ma'at is where the workers live." I turned to the crowd gathering outside the walls. "Look! They're expecting me."

With Khepri hanging on to my neck and Miu at my heels, I went out to greet my people.

A burly man with inky fingers stepped forward and bowed. He gripped a staff in one hand and a writing board in the other. "Welcome to Set Ma'at, O Lord of the Powerful Paw. We were honored to hear from Pharaoh that you were coming to visit us."

"Hey, I remember him," I whispered to Khepri and Miu. "It's the Scribe of the Tomb."

Have you ever met a Scribe of the Tomb? Unless you have a tomb of your own, probably not. Here's how it works: When Pharaoh and the Vizier send orders to the tomb workers, it's the Scribe of the Tomb who reads them and writes back. He tells the Pharaoh and Vizier their orders have been received, and he notifies them of any problems. It's also his job to record everything that happens on the tomb site: every chisel borrowed, every absent worker, every payment made.

Pharaoh also has guards in the Valley of the Kings. Their leader is the Captain of the Guard, and they watch over the tombs under construction, as well as the completed and sealed tombs. But it's the Scribe who oversees the workers themselves. And there are a lot of them. To build a tomb, you need foremen, carpenters, stonemasons, plasterers, sculptors, goldsmiths, painters, and other artisans—and the Scribe keeps track of them all.

In short, the Scribe of the Tomb has a lot of power, and this particular Scribe was the boss of Set Ma'at.

His voice still booming, the Scribe bent down to Miu and the Vizier. "And welcome to the Lord of the Powerful Paw's honorable escort."

Instead of replying, the Vizier focused on the crowd. "Look at you all, standing idle. Why aren't you working?"

"Exactly what I was about to say, my lord," the Scribe said smoothly. "Yesterday we had our annual holiday feast to celebrate the ancient founder of Set Ma'at, but today we must get back to our normal routine—"

"You took another holiday?" the Vizier growled at the crowd. "That's not what Pharaoh pays you for."

The crowd murmured, and a gaunt man stepped forward with a paintbrush in his hand. "O Great Vizier, speaking of payment, perhaps now is the time to remind you that our wages of bread and beer were late last month, and the month before, and the month before that."

There was a murmur of agreement from the back of the crowd, but the Scribe nudged the man with his staff. "That's enough, Pentu."

Pentu didn't stop. "And our pay has been cut, even though we are worked harder—"

"Who gave you permission to speak?" The Vizier was so angry he almost spat out the words. "If I hear you complaining about wages again, you're fired." He turned on the crowd. "And that goes for the rest of you, too."

Everyone went quiet. Pentu hunched his shoulders, and his paintbrush dropped to the ground. A skinny boy behind him picked it up and silently handed it back to him.

"You heard the honored Vizier, everyone," the Scribe boomed. "Back to work!" He pointed to a strapping young man near Pentu. "Except for you, Huya."

Clearly pleased to be singled out, Huya smirked and flexed his muscles. "Want me to make sure that troublemaker Pentu keeps his mouth shut, my lord Scribe? Just say the word—"

"Not just now, Huya." The Scribe ushered him over to the Vizier. "My lord, this is the carpenter Huya, the one I mentioned in my last letter. He's been assisting me with various duties."

"Indeed?" The Vizier gave Huya a piercing

glance. "I hear you're quite capable. And discreet."

Huya's smirk widened as he bowed low. "I'm quiet as a tomb, my lord Vizier."

"Huya has set up a place for you inside the village gates," the Scribe explained to the Vizier. "I had him build the platform in the cool of the wall, where the light is good. You need only escort Pharaoh's Cat there, and our best artists will begin their work."

The Vizier didn't even look at me. Snapping his fingers, he called the nearest boy over, the skinny one who had picked up Pentu's paintbrush. "You, there. Carry the cat where he's supposed to go."

"But—"

"Don't argue!" the Vizier barked.

Shoulders tense, the boy bent down to me. He was about the age of Pharaoh's oldest son—eleven or so, with long fingers, a long neck, and alert, hungry eyes.

"He looks like Pentu, don't you think?" Khepri whispered.

"Hmmm. Yes," I agreed. If they were related, no wonder the Vizier made him tense.

Once the Vizier swept past, the boy smiled at me and held out his arms. "O Gracious Pharaoh's Cat, if you would do me the honor—"

I'm not thrilled about being carried by strangers. But I didn't want the boy to get in trouble, so I let him scoop me up.

To my relief, he knew exactly what he was doing. Honestly, the boy could have a job as an official cat carrier.

"My mother liked cats," he whispered to me. "I don't remember much about her, but I do remember that. So I like them, too."

Moments later, we entered the village gate. Inside its high outer walls, Set Ma'at was just as cramped and busy as I remembered, with dusty houses packed tight together. Water carriers and workmen jostled in narrow, noisy alleys that smelled of wood fires and kitchen scraps.

"Ah!" The Scribe caught up to us. "Kenamon, I see you've made the acquaintance of Pharaoh's Cat already. Very good!" He ushered us toward a platform near the gate. "Now set him down on that pedestal there—the one in the sunshine that Huya set up—and get out your tablet and paint box. I expect to see some very fine work from you today."

As Kenamon settled me on my pedestal, I stared up at him in surprise. This boy was my portrait painter?

CHAPTER 4

Trouble

If I was surprised, so was the Vizier. As he sat down near my pedestal, he said, "That child is far too young for the job, Scribe. What is he, ten?"

"Almost twelve, my lord," the Scribe said. "And the best painter I have ever seen. He began working in the tombs last year, and last month I hired him myself, to paint my dear pet Menwi."

Setting down his staff and writing board, he seated himself and offered the Vizier sweetmeats and wine. The wine didn't interest me, but it smelled like there was spiced goose on that tray, and that was enough to drive me wild. Would anyone think to offer me some?

Not the Vizier. Popping a morsel into his mouth, he stared hard at the artist boy, who was unpacking materials from a box on the ground. "He looks like that troublemaker. The one in the crowd."

"They are father and son," the Scribe admitted, "but the boy has never caused any difficulties." He let his voice drop, but that was no problem for me. Cats hear *everything*. "The father spent too much on medicine when his wife was ill, so they struggle. But that is to our advantage, my lord. To make extra money, the boy will undertake almost any commission in his spare time. You could hire him to do work for your own tomb, my lord, and at very cheap rates—"

"You interest me, Scribe. Let us see what the boy can do." Still staring at Kenamon, the Vizier selected another morsel from the plate.

When the Scribe scoffed a piece, too, I mewed softly, but they ignored me.

"At first, I expect the boy will make only sketches," the Scribe said. "The painting will come later. But it will be marvelous, I promise you."

Huya had been chatting quietly with another carpenter. Now he came up to the Scribe and bowed. The smirk was back again, and he had the air of someone bursting with a secret. "If I might have a quick word, my lord Scribe? And with you, too, my lord Vizier—"

I missed what he had to say because another well-built man, his fingers coated in clay, came up and bowed to *me*. He was older than Huya, and I was pleased to see no trace whatsoever of a smirk on his face. His deep-set eyes were serious, but I saw kindness there.

He laid a leathery scrap of dried pork in front of me. "O Great Pharaoh's Cat, Lord of the Powerful Paw, I am the sculptor Bek. I am honored to have been given the task of carving your statue. Please accept my offering."

To be honest, dried pork doesn't meet my usual snack standards. But the Vizier had just snarfed up the last of the spiced goose, so I gave Bek points for trying.

"You're going to eat that?" Khepri said in surprise as I bit into it.

"Just to be polite," I said.

The pork wasn't as awful as I feared. Maybe the desert air had improved it. Or maybe I was just hungry.

When I licked my lips, Bek smiled at me. "Now, Great Pharaoh's Cat, I must begin my work. If you could just sit up?" He put out his hands to arrange me, but I got there before him, tucking my hindquarters and raising my head high.

Bek beamed at me. "Yes, that's perfect."

Retreating to a table that had been set up for him, he began shaping a lump of clay that was almost exactly the size of my head. I looked from him to Pentu and back again. Both of them were completely focused on me. How wonderful!

"Hold that pose," Bek breathed, and I went still.

"Bek's work will be a wonder," the Scribe said to the Vizier. "He's the finest sculptor in Set Ma'at, as his father was before him, and his father's father, all the way down his line. For centuries, every Pharaoh has chosen the family to work on his tomb."

I kept my face as serene as possible, hoping Bek could see how I resembled my illustrious ancestor, the cat goddess Bastet.

"Hey, look at what Kenamon's doing!" Khepri propped himself on my ear for a better view. "It looks just like you, Ra."

Oh, the agony! I wanted to see the sketch-in-progress, but to get a decent portrait and sculpture I had to stay motionless.

I let out a tiny mewl of frustration. Almost as if he understood, the boy Kenamon tilted his tablet so I could see.

"Look," Khepri whispered joyfully. "He's put me in there, too."

It was indeed a portrait of both of us— and what a portrait it was. Not only had the boy conveyed my innate majesty, but he'd made Khepri look like he really *was* a mark of divine favor. Quite a feat, if you ask me.

As Kenamon went back to work, a barrel-chested man strode past Huya the carpenter, who scowled at him. Twirling his fingers, which were covered with rings, the stranger swept a fancy bow in front of the Vizier. "Neferhotep the goldsmith, my lord. I'm here to copy the collar of Pharaoh's Cat."

"Copy it?" The Vizier frowned. "Why?"

Neferhotep twiddled his fingers again. "So that his statue can be properly decorated, my lord. May I remove the collar now?"

I stifled a wail. That strand of gold and beads was a gift from Pharaoh himself. I'd had it since I was a kitten.

"If that's what you need to do, then do it," the Vizier ordered. "Immediately. We don't have all day."

Neferhotep's restless fingers twitched in my fur, and the collar fell away.

Without it, I didn't quite feel like my-self. Not that anyone seemed to notice. Certainly not Miu, who appeared beneath my pedestal.

"Well, now that Ra is settled in, maybe you and I will go explore," she said to Khepri.

"Sure." Khepri hopped down to her. "Next stop, the Valley of the Kings!"

"Wait," I said through my half-frozen mouth. "You were going to entertain me, remember?"

"We'll tell you all about our adventures when we get back," Khepri said cheerfully.

A moment later, they were gone, and I was miffed. How could my friends leave me alone like this?

But as I sat there feeling sorry for my-self, I wasn't as alone as I thought.

"Wowee. Is that perfume I smell?" An enormous, tiger-striped tomcat swaggered into sight. Brushing past Bek, who smiled down at him, he sauntered up to my pedes-tal. "Well, if it isn't Lord Fancypaws himself, right here in Set Ma'at."

Lord Fancypaws? Was he talking about *me*?

I couldn't do much to put him in his place, not when I needed to hold my pose, but I let my fur rise, to show him who was boss. "The correct title is Pharaoh's Cat, Lord of the Powerful Paw."

"You don't say?" The cat's voice was rough around the edges, but he had presence, and his green eyes were laughing at me. "We desert cats don't pay too much attention to titles."

"And who are you?" I asked.

"I'm Sabu. I'm the leader around here, Fancypaws."

"The name is Pharaoh's Cat," I corrected him, between gritted teeth.

Before I could say more, Miu ran up to me, Khepri clinging to her neck fur. "Ra, I was just talking to some local cats, and I heard the most wonderful news." Seeing Sabu, she stopped. "Oh my goodness, it's true. Sabu, what are you doing here?"

"Miu?" Sabu sounded pleased as could be. "It's been too long."

I stared in dismay as they touched whiskers in greeting. "Miu, you know this cat?"

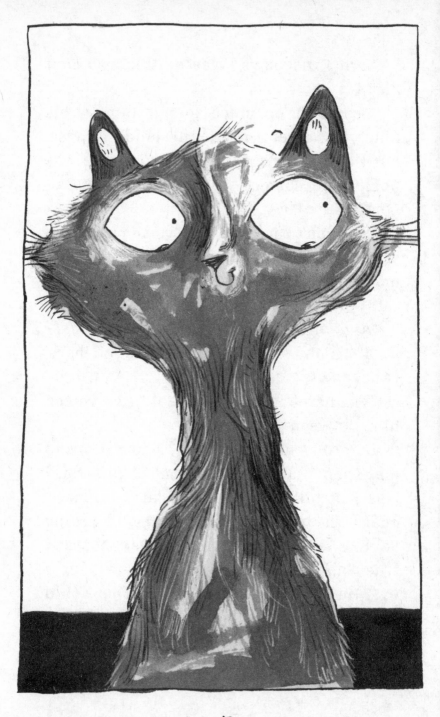

Sabu

"Of course, Ra." She gave Sabu a fond look. "He's my cousin."

"Seventh cousin, twice removed, on our mothers' side," Sabu confirmed. (Cats care about details like that.)

"But we haven't seen each other since I was a tiny kitten," Miu added, touching her whiskers to Sabu's again. "The last I knew, Sabu, you were going out into the world to seek adventure."

"And you were headed off to the palace," Sabu said. "I've always wondered how that worked out."

"I've been happy there," Miu told him. "As you can see, I found friends. And you've made your home here?"

"I live with Bek, the best craftsman in the village." Sabu tilted his head toward the sculptor.

I couldn't help challenging him. "Kenamon's pretty good, too, from what I've seen."

"Kenamon?" Sabu dismissed this. "He's good, but he's just a kid. He likes to monkey around. Bek is a master of his craft." He looked back at the sculptor with affection.

"I know what I'm talking about. I've been with him for years now."

"I'd love to hear more," Miu said. "If you've got time, maybe you could show us the area? Khepri and I thought we might visit the Valley of the Kings, but we weren't sure which path to take."

Before Sabu could reply, there was a commotion outside the gate. It sounded like a crowd was gathering.

"What's going on?" the Vizier demanded. "It had better not be another party, Scribe."

"No, my lord." The Scribe turned to the carpenter, who was still by his side. "Huya, put a stop to this. Tell them the Vizier is displeased."

Huya was in midstride when the crowd came through the gate. At their head was a young guard in a dusty loincloth, carrying a sharp spear.

"My lords!" The guard stumbled toward the Scribe and the Vizier. "A tomb has been robbed!"

CHAPTER 5

Protector of the Dead

"Tomb robbers!" I jumped off my pedestal, tail bristling. "Let me at them!"

If there's anything lower than a tomb robber, I don't know what it is. Ordinary thieves are bad enough, but tomb robbers mess up your afterlife. I'm talking eternal damage. It's beyond despicable.

Tail still on high alert, I pointed myself toward the gate. "I'll track them down, wherever they are. They'll learn not to cross Ra the Mighty—"

"Hush, Ra!" Miu cut me off. "Listen to the guard."

"It's true, my lords!" The guard's spear shook. "I tell you, the god Anubis was seen in the Valley last night. He attacked our men, and then he entered a tomb."

The Scribe and the Vizier both turned pale, and so did Kenamon. Huya stopped smirking, and Neferhotep's hands shook. The sculptor Bek even went so far as to snatch up Sabu in his arms, as if to protect him.

Anubis has that effect on people. He's the jackal-headed guide of the afterlife, the protector of the dead, the weigher of souls. Of all the gods in Egypt, he's the spookiest.

But I'd never heard of him robbing a tomb before.

"Isn't Anubis supposed to *guard* the tombs?" I whispered to Miu and Khepri.

"He certainly is," Miu agreed. "If you ask me, the whole story sounds fishy. Why would Anubis rob a tomb? It's humans who do that. I wonder what really happened."

"It's a Great Mystery!" Khepri said gleefully. "Even you can't deny it this time, Ra."

It was true. I couldn't. Though part of me wished I could. There was always the chance that Anubis *was* involved, and he's one god you don't want to mess with.

"Er . . . maybe we should let the Vizier handle this," I said.

"The Vizier?" Khepri slid down Miu's fur and landed at my feet. "Ra, it's a royal tomb robbery. And you're Pharaoh's Cat. You have a responsibility here."

My tail was no longer bristling, but I had to admit he was right. A royal tomb robbery was exactly the kind of case Pharaoh's Cat ought to take. "All right, all right," I conceded. "We'll investigate. For a bit, anyway."

"Hooray!" Khepri raced up to my head. "Quick! The guard's taking the Vizier and the Scribe to the scene of the crime. Huya's going, too. Let's go with them."

In the end, we hitched a ride on the Vizier's litter. Not that the Vizier approved.

"Stay out of my way, you beasts," he grunted.

Ignoring him, I dug my claws into a prize cushion and watched the sculptor Bek stroke Sabu and hand-feed him small morsels. Sabu took them like a ruler accepting tribute.

41

Probably just more bits of dried-up pork, I told myself. Nothing that could excite the discerning palate of Pharaoh's Cat. But my stomach growled anyway. *How come Sabu's getting snacks and I'm not?*

I turned as the Scribe approached, hoping he would refill my snack bowls. Instead he pushed Kenamon toward us. "Take the boy with you, Vizier. He can draw pictures of the damage to the tomb. I'll need them for my records and reports."

The Vizier looked down his nose at Kenamon. "Can't he walk with you, Scribe?"

"The guard and I can keep up with you, and so can Huya," the Scribe said. "But the boy will slow us down."

"Very well." The Vizier gestured for Kenamon to board. "Sit with the cats, boy."

Kenamon seemed pleased to join us. For his benefit, I struck a magnificent pose and held it. The boy reached for his paint box, and I saw admiration in his eyes.

It was almost as good as a snack.

We were halfway down the Valley of

the Kings when I realized that something terrible had happened. "My collar!" I meowed in distress. "We left it in Set Ma'at."

"Don't worry," Khepri said. "It's not like it's missing. Neferhotep is looking after it."

That didn't make me feel any better. My necklace wasn't supposed to be in the goldsmith's twitchy hands. It was supposed to be on my neck.

"It's probably safer in Set Ma'at, anyway," Miu pointed out. "If you lost it in these cliffs, you'd never find it again."

"You're missing the point," I protested. "That collar is part of me. It was a gift from Pharaoh."

Miu looked askance at me. "You know, Ra, cats don't *need* jewelry."

"This one does," I said miserably. *Oh, slender gold chain! Oh, little gold beads that go clink!* "If you had any yourself, you'd understand."

"Well, I don't," Miu said. "And somehow I survive."

"Same here," Khepri chirped. "Cheer up, Ra."

I wasn't consoled, and when we reached

the site of the attack, I felt even worse. It was so hot my fur almost blistered.

"Ouch!" I picked up my paws as fast as I put them down. "Ouch! Ouch! Ouch!"

From his perch between my ears, Khepri urged me on. "Follow Miu. She's doing just fine."

"Miu's a kitchen cat," I told him. "She's used to heat."

"You'll get used to it, too," Khepri assured me.

Easy for him to say. He wasn't the one scorching his paws on the oven-hot cliffs.

One more painful step, and then I was saved: Kenamon scooped me up. "Forgive the liberty, Ra the Mighty, but you look like you need help."

It was a liberty, and in ordinary circumstances I couldn't have permitted it. But as it was, I forgave him right away. What a thoughtful boy!

Lolling in Kenamon's arms, I asked Khepri, "Who's that between the Vizier and the Scribe? He looks just like Huya."

Well, not exactly alike, since this man was half a head taller and his mouth wasn't twisted in a smirk. Still, the resemblance was strong.

"That's the Captain of the Guard," Khepri told me. "Shhh. He's talking about the attack."

In his rumpled uniform, the Captain looked as if he'd been up all night. "That's where we found the guards, left for dead," he said, pointing up the cliff.

"When did they go missing?" the Scribe asked. He had propped his staff between two rocks, and he was jotting down notes on his writing board.

The Captain rubbed his nose, looking embarrassed. "It's . . . er . . . hard to say. Things were a bit irregular last night, what with the holiday and the feast."

"I don't believe it." The Vizier looked outraged. "Is there anyone in this place who believes in doing his job?"

"Oh, we went out on patrol, my lord," the Captain said hastily. "We're short-staffed right now, but we know our duty. It's just that we thought those two guards were taking shelter from the sandstorm that hit in the small hours of the night. When they were still absent this morning, we sent out a search party. They were in bad shape when we found them."

"And what's all this about Anubis?" the Vizier asked.

"Both men say they saw the god right before they were struck, my lord. And one saw treasure in the god's hands."

The Vizier's eyes narrowed. "I want to question them."

"They're not here, my lord," the Captain said patiently. "They're recovering from their injuries at the guard post—"

"Send for them," the Vizier barked. "*Now.*"

After the Captain reluctantly gave the order, the Scribe asked, "Which tomb was robbed?"

"I can't say for certain," the Captain admitted. "The sandstorm has covered up any footprints, and the entrance seals are intact on every tomb we've checked so far. There's no damage anywhere. But we found this." He pulled a gold ring from his pouch and passed it to the Scribe. "I think I've read the writing on it properly, but I'm no expert."

The Scribe examined it. "This is from the tomb of Setnakht."

Setnakht? That was one of my Pharaoh's distinguished forefathers, owner of Pamiu, my ancestor. Both Setnakht and Pamiu had been legends in their day, and the sarcophagus that held Pamiu's mummy was supposed to be legendary, too. Fashioned from gold and wood, it was said to resemble a living cat, with golden fur and eyes of glowing amber.

"Setnakht, eh?" The Captain nodded. "I thought that's what it said. We checked his tomb, and it's still sealed tight, but someone must have found another way in. We'll need to open the seals and see what else has been stolen—with your permission, my lords."

Instead of answering, the Scribe passed the ring to the Vizier.

The Vizier clenched the ring in his fist. "Captain, how can you ask us to disturb Setnakht's sacred place of rest? For all we know, this ring never entered the tomb. Perhaps it was misplaced when Setnakht was buried, more than a century ago."

"It was found out in the open, near one of the attacked men," the Captain said. "It's unlikely it's been sitting there for a century, my lord. This area is patrolled regularly, and work crews pass through here. And gold catches the light."

The Vizier scowled. The Scribe crossed out something on his writing board.

"No one wishes to violate the sacred seals of a tomb," the Captain went on. "But if a robbery is suspected, we must act. If you cannot give permission, I must go to Pharaoh himself."

The Vizier reddened, though I couldn't tell if it was with embarrassment or anger. "Very well," he snapped. "Open the tomb."

If the Vizier was red-faced to begin with, he turned positively purple when they finally unsealed the tomb. Our eyes had barely adjusted to the dim torchlight in the inner chamber when he began wailing.

"Thieves! Traitors! Heretics! They've disturbed Setnakht's eternal rest! They've robbed him of his treasures!"

From my perch in Kenamon's arms, I stared in shock at the tomb.

It was a wreck.

The thieves had stripped the statues of their gold. They'd hacked at the gilded furniture, probably to get jewels. Worst of all, they'd pried open the enormous stone sarcophagus that held Setnakht's mummy, and they'd yanked off his priceless amulets and collar.

"They even took his heart scarab," Khepri said softly, looking at the mummy's bare chest.

Placed on a mummy's heart, the scarab-shaped stone was supposed to ease his way into the afterlife. Setnakht's heart scarab would have been large, and probably made of jasper or amethyst. Very valuable, in short.

"Sacrilege!" the Vizier screamed, and I had to agree.

But then, when I jumped down to the floor, I saw something even worse.

"Khepri!" I cried "Miu!"

Miu rushed to my side.

Khepri clutched at my fur. "What is it, Ra?"

I pointed with a trembling paw. "Look!" I had to shield my own eyes from the sight. "My great ancestor Pamiu—that's his mummy dumped on the floor. The robbers stole his golden sarcophagus!"

CHAPTER 6

On the Hunt

I forced myself to look again at the help-less cat mummy. The ears were broken, the bandages loose. Across time and space, I seemed to hear Pamiu's voice: *Avenge me, Ra the Mighty. See that justice is done.*

How could I ignore a call like that?

"The Great Detective is on the case," I promised out loud.

Khepri coughed. "Great Detectives, you mean."

"That's right," Miu agreed. "We're a team."

True. We'd settled on that after our last case. "But this feels personal," I told them. "It's *my* ancestor lying there. So it's my duty to take charge."

"We're in this together." Swishing her tail,

Miu stepped toward Pamiu's desecrated mummy. "Do you think I'm not upset, Ra? A cat is a cat."

"But this cat was special," I reminded her. "After all, not every Pharaoh's Cat gets a golden sarcophagus. That honor is granted only to the very best, and the most beloved." In a low voice, I confessed, "To tell the truth, I'm kind of hoping for one myself."

Miu sighed and glanced up at Khepri, and I went back to staring at Pamiu's poor tattered mummy. No doubt the robbers would strip his wonderful sarcophagus of its amber eyes and melt down the rest for the gold.

The humans took a while to catch up to us, but eventually the Scribe discovered Pamiu's mummy. "Vizier, look at this. The cat's sarcophagus was stolen, too. Another priceless object gone!"

"Make a list, Scribe. Make a list." Recovering from his initial outrage, the Vizier roved around the burial chamber. "Put down everything missing, everything that looks out of place. And above all, find where the thieves broke in. We can't catch them till we know how they did the job."

Instead of sitting down with his writing board, the Scribe jabbed his staff at Kenamon. "You there. Start sketching. I want a record of all the damage we see."

"There's no sign of entry anywhere," the Captain said, still scanning the walls. "I don't understand how they did it."

As he lowered his flaming torch, the chamber darkened, creating a distinctly spooky atmosphere.

"*Anoooooooooooooobis.*" It was the faintest breath of a whisper, but my fur stood on end when I heard it. Everyone stopped in their tracks, and the Vizier and the Scribe stared at each other wild-eyed.

Miu nudged me. She was watching Kenamon, and I noticed he was the one human who didn't look scared. He even had a twinkle in his eyes. I remembered how Sabu had said the boy liked to monkey around. Did that mean he played jokes? Was he the whisperer? Or was it the god of the dead, warning us away?

I glanced back at the tunnel entrance,

then gasped in alarm. Two stiff-legged figures were coming toward us, moaning a little, their cloth wrappings fluttering in the eerie light of the flames.

"Mummies!" Wailing, I darted behind a canopic jar.

"Vizier," said the Captain, "these are the guards who were attacked on the cliffs."

Oh.

"An easy mistake to make," I told Khepri, who was chortling on top of my head. "All those bandages are very misleading."

I came out of hiding.

"Tell the Vizier what happened to you," the Captain prompted the men.

Nursing his arm in a sling, the taller man kept his head bent, as if it pained him. "We were out on patrol together, my lord. It was a moonless night, so it wasn't an easy job. But we had the stars." He stopped and bit his lip.

"Go on," said the Captain.

The man's head drooped even lower. "Just after midnight, we heard jackals howling in this canyon. They don't usually make that much noise, so we thought we'd better investigate. And then they turned on us—dozens of jackals, all at once, running straight for us and splitting us up. I climbed to get away from them, but when I turned . . ." The man shut his eyes, as if he didn't want to remember.

"What?" the Vizier demanded.

"I saw a huge jackal's head." The petrified man could barely get the words out. "It was the god Anubis, and he was angry. And that's the last thing I remember."

The shorter man had a bandaged head

and a tightly wrapped leg. "I ran, too, my lord. But then I heard a cry. That's when I saw the great god Anubis, rising up before me, his hands full of gold and jewels." His voice shook at the memory. "The p-power of the god overcame me, and he wiped my mind blank. The rest is gone."

The Vizier looked unnerved. So did the Scribe. To tell the truth, I was feeling a little unnerved myself.

I looked at Kenamon. He seemed as spooked as the rest of us. The twinkle was gone.

"I don't know what to think." The Captain glanced around the tomb uneasily. "We questioned the men separately, of course, but the details match. And they both swear their testimony is true."

The torch flickered, and the chamber grew darker still. In the uncanny setting, it was easy to imagine a dark, wolfish face looming against the night sky. As the silence stretched out, you could almost hear the jackal god's stealthy footsteps coming our way.

I shivered. Khepri dropped down to the

floor, as if he needed the comfort of solid ground beneath him. Even Miu looked unsettled.

"Could it be true?" The Captain's voice was hushed. "Does Anubis walk this Valley?"

The Vizier stared at the wall painting beside him, of the black-headed jackal god weighing the hearts of the dead. My eyes were fixed on it, too.

"The tomb was sealed." The Vizier sounded faint. "And we have found no other entrance."

"Only a god could enter," the Scribe whispered.

He and the Vizier gave each other a long, uncertain look.

"I need fresh air." Pressing a hand to his sweaty forehead, the Vizier stumbled toward the tunnel. With a shudder, the Scribe followed him out, gripping his staff tightly and clutching his writing board close to his chest.

I crouched down, trying to avoid the golden eyes of the Anubis painting.

No one is braver than Pharaoh's Cat, of course. My friends always say so. (Well, not

Khepri and Miu. But everyone else.) Yet a god is a god, and a cat's powers can hardly compare. Our purr can make you humans talk, but that's all we have. And that isn't much help when you're dealing with the guardian of the afterlife.

"Honestly, this whole Anubis business gives me the creeps," I said to Miu and Khepri. "How about we leave right now?"

Khepri clicked at me in reproof. "We're Great Detectives, Ra. We don't let our fears get the better of us. We search out the truth."

"That's right," Miu agreed. "We need to look for evidence—cold, hard facts."

"Fine," I said, still crouching. "How about we look for them outside?"

"Ra, if we go out, they might not let us back in," Khepri said. "We need to search this tomb while we can."

"If you're scared, you don't have to stay," Miu said reassuringly. "We'll get the job done and meet you outside."

"Who's scared?" I forced myself to stand up. If anyone was going to avenge Pamiu, it was going to be me. "It's just that it's kind of dark in here, and stuffy." *And spooky.*

"Let's see if we can work out how the robbers got in." Khepri scrambled toward the corner of the room. "Check the walls, especially down low. Oh, and the floors. Humans never pay proper attention to floors."

The Captain and his men and Huya were examining the main chamber and the tunnel that led to it, but Khepri was right: they weren't paying much attention to anything below their knees. Only Kenamon seemed to be inspecting everything, and he was making very slow work of it.

Khepri, Miu, and I got down to business. We paced the perimeter of the chamber, keeping out of the way of the humans, sniffing (me and Miu) and scuttling (Khepri) as we went.

We were under a gilded chair, examining a section of floor the humans had skipped over, when I said, "You know, this is hard work."

Miu pressed her nose to a crack between two stones.

"The kind of work that makes you hungry," I said.

Click, click, click, went Khepri.

"The kind of work," I said dreamily, "that makes you wish you had a bowl of spiced ibex right in front of you." I closed my eyes, imagining it. "Seasoned with cumin, and just a touch of cinnamon. I tell you, I can practically smell it right now."

"That's funny." Miu sat up, alert. "I can smell cinnamon, too."

"Aha!" Khepri pounced. "Look at this!"

He waved a tiny crumb above his head.

"Our first clue," he announced.

CHAPTER 7

A Hole in the Wall

Miu and I sniffed at Khepri's find.

"It's a smidgen of spiced meat. Goose, maybe?" Miu theorized.

"Yes," I agreed. "Heavy on the cinnamon, with a dusting of cumin. Not what they'd serve at the palace, but not bad, either. And it smells pretty fresh, too."

"If you ask me, it smells *disgusting*," Khepri said, backing away from it. "Honestly, I don't know how anyone can choke that stuff down. Especially when you could be eating dung instead."

"Look on the bright side," I told him. "It means more dung for you."

"That's true." Khepri brightened. "Hey, I think there's another bit by the wall."

Miu retrieved it, and we took a look. It was just like the other one, only a little bigger and stickier.

"Well, I think we can rule out Anubis as the thief," Miu said.

"Unless Anubis eats cinnamon-spiced goose," I added.

"Unlikely," Khepri said, and I had to agree.

Miu was sniffing at a half-column in the wall behind the chair. "You know, this smells like cinnamon, too."

"What does?" Khepri asked.

"I'm not sure," Miu admitted. "It's almost as if the smell is coming from the place where the column joins with the wall."

Khepri and I went over to have a look and a sniff.

"That's interesting," Khepri said. "The mortar's loose there. See?" He started scrabbling.

Miu and I were watching him closely when my ears swiveled in alarm.

I backed away from the wall. "Miu? I've got a bad feeling . . ."

"Not Anubis again." She didn't even look around.

"No." My tail twitched. "It's a—"

The chamber erupted in barking as a gray beast barreled toward us, shattering a row of canopic jars. A guard pulled at the beast's leash. "He's found something!"

"DOG!" I screeched as the beast sprang forward.

"No!" Kenamon shouted, leaping up. "Stop!"

Khepri pulled out of sight. Miu and I leaped onto the back of the chair, claws at the ready. *Hissssssssssss!*

As Kenamon jumped in front of us, the gray dog reared up, brought to heel by the leash.

"It's just two cats," the guard said, disappointed.

"It's Pharaoh's Cat," Kenamon explained to the guard. "And his friend."

The dog hung his head. "Whoops," he muttered. "Guess I got a little overexcited."

"Get that dog out of here," the Captain ordered from the other side of the room. "This place is enough of a wreck as it is. We don't need any more damage."

As the guard dragged at the leash, the dog waggled his perky ears at me in farewell. "Didn't realize you were Pharaoh's Cat. Sorry about that."

"Whew!" I said to Miu, after the dog had gone. "That was a close call."

"I don't see Khepri," Miu said anxiously.

"Khepri?" I leaped down to look for him. "Hey, buddy, are you there?"

Khepri popped out from behind the half-column, covered with debris. "I've found it!" He waved his forelegs in triumph. "I've found the way in!" He pointed to the tiny hole in the wall behind him. "There!"

Miu studied the hole. "A way in for a beetle, maybe," she said. "But a human's a little bigger, Khepri."

"Wait!" A thought struck me. Maybe I

had cracked the case. "What if the robbers were *beetles*?"

"Ra, that doesn't make any sense." Khepri dusted himself off. "Anyway, I've found a way in for humans. This whole big block by the column is loose. Someone's recently packed it back in. And get this: there's a hole behind it, and then another loose block. And if you get around *that* block—which you can, because it's been moved, too—then you're in a different tomb. An abandoned one."

"Are you sure?" I crouched down to look, but all I could see was the tiny hole.

"Of course I'm sure," Khepri said indignantly.

"Then we need to let the humans know," Miu said. "I think Kenamon already suspects something."

I looked up and saw the boy staring down at us, and at the tiny hole.

"Maybe he'll bring the other humans over," Khepri said.

But the boy turned away and said nothing.

"I think he didn't understand," Miu said.

"Then you two need to bring the other humans over," Khepri said. "I'll help, if I can."

Miu raced over to the Captain and rubbed against his shins. I sauntered in front of him, pointing my tail toward the wall. He waved us away. Honestly, humans are terrible at communication.

Next we tried standing by the wall and meowing.

"Put those cats out!" the Captain ordered. "I've had enough of their antics."

The next thing we knew, the guards had kicked us out of the tomb.

"Well, how do you like that?" Blinking in the bright sunlight, I nudged down my fur where the guards had ruffled it. "We were only trying to help."

Miu was licking herself clean. "I'm afraid those humans don't deserve us."

"No, they don't," Khepri agreed. "But we're not going to let them keep the Great Detectives from cracking this case. Let's find that abandoned tomb I saw. I didn't get a chance to check it for clues."

We picked our way past the Vizier and the Scribe, who were whispering and glaring at each other.

"The other tomb should be below and to the north of this one," Khepri said, urging me down the cliffside. "At least that's my guess."

"There." Miu bobbed her head. "That cleft in the rocks. Could that be it?"

I darted forward. "Let's find out."

Sure enough, it was the entrance to a tomb.

"There's nothing to stop us just walking in," Miu said as we entered the dark tunnel. "The seal is missing."

"Probably because thieves damaged it beyond repair," I said. "That's the usual reason."

As we left sunlight far behind, I started to feel jumpy.

"Don't worry," Khepri said. "It'll get light again when we get to the burial chamber."

"No, it won't." I set him straight. "The whole point of a burial chamber is that it's buried, Khepri. As in, *underground*. As in, *no light*."

"This one has light," Khepri insisted.

"Nonsense," I said.

But he was right. There was a hole in the burial chamber roof. It had been patched up with a slab of stone that didn't quite fit, so bright sunlight poured in around the edges.

Miu climbed up a wide, half-broken ledge to get a better look. "The hole doesn't look new," she reported. "I guess that's how the original robbers got in."

"And then they burned the place." The tomb had been swept out, but I could smell the soot. "They do that sometimes, after they ransack the treasure. It gets rid of the evidence." Not that I'd ever actually seen a tomb robber set fire to anything. But you learn a lot when you sit in Pharaoh's lap, listening to his viziers drone on.

Khepri slid down my back and tail to the floor and scuttled over to the nearest wall. "There! What did I tell you?" He tapped a block that was not quite aligned with the others. "That's the block that was moved."

"And here's another bit of dried meat," said Miu, her nose to the ground.

"So many clues!" I was pleased. "We'll have this case cracked before you know it."

"I'm not sure." Miu sounded worried. "First we have to get the humans in here. And then we have to get them to pay attention. I don't know how we're going to do that."

I didn't like to admit it, but neither did I.

"I've got an idea," Khepri said.

"What is it?" I asked.

"You're fast, aren't you, Ra?"

"As fast as they come," I said modestly.

"And clever?"

"As clever as they—" I stopped and narrowed my eyes at Khepri. "Wait a minute. What are you asking me to do?"

CHAPTER 8

An Inside Job

"You should get the dog to chase you," Khepri said. "Lure him into the tomb."

I blinked. "You want that beast to chase me?"

"Yes," Khepri said cheerily. "If he corners you in here, then the guards will have to come in to sort things out. They'll see that the block is out of place, and then—"

"And then I'll be that dog's dinner," I finished. "I can't believe you're suggesting this, Khepri. Did you see his teeth?"

"He'll never catch you, Ra. You're too fast for that. And too clever."

"I'm clever enough to say no," I told him.

Khepri went on as if I hadn't spoken. "You'd leap up on that half-broken ledge, and the guards would rescue you, and then they'd give you snacks to revive you—"

"Snacks?" I reconsidered my position. "You think they'd do that?"

"Of course," Khepri said. "You'll be half fainting in their arms, and it will be their dog's fault. They'll *have* to make it up to you. You're Pharaoh's Cat."

"Hmmm . . ." I thought this over. "Well, all right then. But I'm not doing this alone, Khepri. You have to sit on my head and be the lookout."

"Done." Khepri scrambled up to my head. "Now let's plan our attack—"

"We'll come in from the side," I suggested.

"A head-on attack would be better," Khepri maintained.

"Head-on? With a dog? Khepri—"

"You two are taking too long." Miu dashed back down the tunnel.

"Hey, wait!" I wasn't going to be robbed of my glory—or my snacks. I bounded after her as fast as I could go.

The momentum carried me out to the cliffside, where I passed Miu and headed straight for the dog.

"Go get him, Ra!" Khepri hollered in my ear.

"You bet I will!" I hollered back.

The gray beast was standing at attention by a clutch of guards. I sideswiped him, kicking up a cloud of dust right under his nose. "Catch me if you can!" I bellowed, and then my feet went out from under me in a scree of loose stones.

I landed right under the dog's nose.

"Yikes!" Khepri shrieked. "Get up, Ra!"

Dazed, I rolled over, but that only gave me a close-up view of the dog's mouth, opening wide. I shut my eyes, sure it was the end.

"Sorry," the dog said gruffly. "But I can't."

I blinked. "What?"

The dog looked abashed. "No offense, Great Pharaoh's Cat. It's kind of you to offer to play a game with me, especially after the way I treated you earlier. But I have to say no. I'm on duty, you see. And besides, I'm on a leash."

"Oh." I sneaked a look. The rope leash blended in with the cliffside, but it was definitely there. As Miu trotted up, I rolled to my feet, just out of leash range. "Er . . . no offense taken. I was . . . trying to be friendly."

"Maybe on my off hours?" the dog said eagerly. "I could play then."

"Er . . ." I stalled for an answer.

"That's too late," Miu whispered to me. "We need help now."

"She's right," Khepri mumbled in my ear. "I think we need a new plan. This one isn't working."

"What's that you're talking about?" the dog asked, cocking his head to one side. "Something about a plan?"

Pharaoh's Cat is a keen judge of character, and up close I could see that this dog was a very obliging sort of fellow. So, then and there, I decided to take him into my confidence.

"You're right, I'm Pharaoh's Cat," I said. "And you are . . . ?"

"Boo," the dog said proudly. "Faithful servant of the Captain of the Guard and his men."

"We have a problem, Boo," I explained. "We've found some clues in another tomb—"

"The one you just came out of?" the dog interrupted.

"Yes."

The dog nodded wisely. "That was the tomb of Thutmose the Second. It was robbed a couple of years ago, but we tracked down the thieves. Of course, they'd melted everything down by then and set fire to what was left, so nothing could be recovered, not even the mummy. But I still think of it as Thutmose the Second's tomb."

"Well, whatever it's called," I said, "we need the humans to go inspect it. Any chance you could help us?"

"I'll see what I can do," Boo said, but he didn't look hopeful. "Truth is, they're not likely to let me off the leash again today, not after the mess I made earlier. And they're too strong for me to drag them all the way there."

When we told Boo what the clues were, he was even less optimistic. "It'll be a job getting them to notice that," he said. "They're not the brightest bunch, humans. And they're worse than usual today, after feasting and drinking so late into the night."

"Did you see what happened?" Miu asked.

"Last night?" Boo scratched himself. "No, I can't say I did. I took advantage of their party to catch up on my sleep. The Captain's had me out on night duty for weeks."

"What about this morning, during the hunt for the missing guards?" Khepri followed up. "Did you notice anything then?"

"Nope. It was just the same old cliffs. There wasn't much to see—"

"Or smell?" Miu asked.

"Not after that sandstorm last night," Boo said. "Blew away all the evidence, I guess.

Anyway, I'm not really a scent hound. I'm a sight hound. I track things with my eyes."

"So you didn't smell the meat in the tomb?" I asked.

Boo licked his muzzle. "There was meat?"

"Only a little," Miu said.

"Goose spiced with cinnamon and a touch of cumin," I added.

"Hmmm." Boo thought this over. "Sounds like the stew from our feast."

"Aha!" Khepri slid down my nose and hopped onto the rocks. "This may be our breakthrough. Who made the stew?"

"The villagers," Boo said. "Goose with cinnamon and a bit of cumin is a Set Ma'at specialty. On big feast days, they always cook up enough for the guards, too. They bring it up to us in big pots. We always finish it all, every scrap."

"So the stew's a village specialty?" Khepri said thoughtfully. "That suggests the tomb robbery is an inside job."

"Yes," I agreed, then whispered to Khepri, "Doesn't it have to be? I mean, you can't rob the outside of a tomb."

"*Inside job* is just an expression, Ra,"

Khepri whispered back. "It means that the robbers come from inside the village. They aren't from somewhere across the Nile or the desert."

"It figures," Boo said glumly. "Lots of tomb robberies are inside jobs. The workers know all the secrets. They remember the layout and location of the tombs, and the treasures inside them, and the traps. Sometimes they even try to copy the traps in their own tombs in the cliffs by the village. But their operations aren't run as well. If they put in a pit to catch thieves, they never make it deep enough, and their spikes are never sharp enough—"

I cut across his mournful tones. "This is great."

"Great?" Miu echoed doubtfully. "I don't see why, Ra."

"We've got this case almost cracked," I said. "All we have to do is find out who had leftover stew, and we'll have our tomb robber. Ta-dah! I bet we'll be back at the palace for midafternoon snacks."

"It might not be that simple, Ra," Khepri said anxiously.

Poor Khepri. He's a worrier by nature. He's lucky he has someone like me to cheer him up.

"It'll be simple, believe me," I said. "All we have to do is get back to the village—"

I glanced around and frowned. The Vizier was nowhere in sight, and neither was his litter.

"Our ride," I said in alarm. "It's gone!"

CHAPTER 9

Stay Away from the Tombs

"That's right," Boo said, beating the ground with his tail. "The Vizier left just before you came over to visit me. He's headed back to Set Ma'at. The Scribe and his man Huya and the boy went, too."

"Without us?" I was scandalized.

"The boy went looking, but he couldn't find you. And the Vizier said he wouldn't wait, and that you'd find your own way back." Boo pointed his muzzle down the Valley. "If you look down there, you can see the litter."

They were so far away that the litter was tinier than one of my toes. But at least it was still in sight.

"Come on!" I scooped Khepri up with my

paw and deposited him on my head. "We don't want to miss our ride."

I raced down the cliffside. My paws burned, but I didn't care. It was either this, or walk the whole way back.

"Ra, you forgot to say good-bye," Miu said, bounding down after me.

I turned and waved to the dog. "Thanks for the help!"

"Come back anytime!" Boo howled after us. "Maybe you . . ."

I didn't catch his last words. I was running too fast.

"Ra, wait!" Miu called.

I didn't slow down, but she overtook me anyway. "You missed an invitation," she said. "To play games at twilight."

"Fat chance." I continued catapulting down the Valley. "I'll be back in the palace by then, and you can bet I won't be leaving it."

"First you have to get to Set Ma'at," Miu pointed out.

"I'm working on it." I stopped on a rocky outcrop, panting from the heat. We'd closed some of the distance between us and the Vizier, but not enough.

"Come on," Miu said. "We'll need to pick up the pace if we're going to catch up with them."

The next time I looked up, the Vizier's litter was even farther away from us than before.

"They're getting faster," I moaned.

"Actually, I think we're getting slower," said Miu. "It's the heat."

"I'll bring you up to speed," cried Khepri. "Forward march! One, two, three, four, one two, three—"

"Here's another idea, Khepri." Stepping on some sharp pebbles, I winced. "Why don't *you* carry *me*?"

Khepri thought that was very funny.

"I'm not joking." The sun was beating my

head like a drum. "I tell you I can't . . . go . . . on."

I expected Miu would say I had to keep running, but she slowed down, too. "I think we need a break," she panted. "Just a short one."

Before she could change her mind, I dropped to the ground, so exhausted I didn't see the dung pile beside me.

"Wow!" Khepri leaped headfirst. "What a great lunch! If we have to stop, then this is the perfect place."

"I refuse to watch," I told him.

"Mmmmmmm," Khepri said blissfully. "This dung has such an intriguing aroma. Not quite dog, I'd say. Wilder than that. But I'm not sure exactly what—"

A howl floated across the canyon.

"Anooooooooooooooooooooobis!"

Khepri scrambled onto my back. "Wh-What was that?"

I leaped up. "I don't know. But I sure hope you wiped your feet."

"Jackals!" shrieked Miu. "Over there!"

"Impossible," I said as she bolted past me. "They don't hunt by day." But when I glanced over my shoulder, I saw them: half a dozen of the golden wolf-kin streaming toward us, fur shining in the sunlight.

"Anooooooooooooooooooooobis!"

Forgetting my exhaustion, I streaked down the hill after Miu, but the dusty terrain offered no cover, and we weren't fast enough. Before we knew it, the jackals had us surrounded, caught in a dip in the path that led back to Set Ma'at.

"Anooooooooooooooooooobis!"

The cry echoed from one baying mouth to another. Ugly laughter followed.

"I hope the joke isn't on us," Khepri whispered.

The jackals were so close that I could see the dark outline around their glowing eyes. The leader of the pack snapped his jaws, and the circle tightened.

"Stay away from the toooooooooombs!" the leader warned us.

"Stay away from the toooooooooombs!" They all took up the cry.

Beside me, Miu was breathing very fast. She didn't look scared anymore, just mad.

"We're not even going to the tombs," she burst out. "If you jackals just paid attention, you'd notice we're on our way back to the village."

"Miu!" I tried to nudge her into silence, but she shook me off.

"So leave us alone," she finished defiantly.

The leader bared sharp teeth set in black gums. "Don't you go giving me orders, cat." He threw back his head and howled again. "Beware the jackals of *Anooooooooooooooooobis!*"

"*Anoooooooooooooooooobis!*" the rest of them bayed.

"What's all this about Anubis, anyway?" Miu demanded. "Do you know something about the tomb robbery?"

The leader's eyes flashed. "You don't get to ask questions, cat."

"Oh, yes, I do," Miu said. "I'm a Great Detective."

I saw the leader's jaw snap. His pack took a step closer.

"That's our game!" I said quickly, making myself look as silly as possible. (It's not easy for Pharaoh's Cat to hide his innate intelligence and savvy, but he can if he has to.) "You've probably played it, too. Detectives and Tomb Robbers? Just us cats having a fun time. With our beetle." I gave him a friendly tail salute. "But we're ready to go home now."

The leader watched me intently.

"Did I mention I'm Pharaoh's Cat?" I added helpfully. "That means I'm under Pharaoh's protection. Not to mention the protection of Bastet and the sun god Ra himself."

The leader got an odd look in his eye. "Pharaoh's Cat, huh?" He conferred with his second-in-command.

"Pharaoh . . . Bastet . . . Ra," I heard them mutter. And then the second-in-command said, "Don't worry, Chief, I hear that cat's not so smart. Spends his time napping."

Hah! Pharaoh's Cat is as smart as they come. I almost spoke out loud, but I remembered in time that I was supposed to be playing dumb.

"All right." The leader motioned to the pack, and they backed off. "Go home, Pharaoh's Pussycat. Take your friends with you. But don't you come around here again." He raised his sharp muzzle to the sky. "Stay away from the tooooooooooooooooooombs!"

"Stay away from the tooooooooombs!" the pack cried.

We didn't move till they'd vanished back into the cliffs. Even then, we could still hear them howling in the distance—and sniggering and laughing.

"Anoooooooooooooooooooobis!"

"Horrible beasts," Miu said angrily. "Who do they think they are?"

"Well, they can't be the robbers," Khepri reasoned. "Not unless they can haul blocks of stone around."

"True. But they know something," Miu said, looking back at the cliffs. "I'm sure of it."

"Let's figure it out later," I begged. "Right now, I just want to get back to Set Ma'at."

The Vizier's litter could no longer be seen. Miu and I had to travel by paw the whole way back, step by painful step, with Khepri keeping time. I'd never walked so far in my life.

"It's not such a big deal, Ra," Miu said. "Why, lots of cats cover this much ground every day."

"Pharaoh's Cat doesn't," I croaked, my voice dried out by the heat. "Pharaoh's Cat gets *carried*."

By the time we reached Set Ma'at, I was barely able to creep through the gates.

"Just take me back to the palace," I whispered. "I'll never leave Pharaoh's side again."

"You don't mean that, Ra," Khepri said.

"Oh, yes, I do." I dragged myself into the shade of a white-pillared house. "Where's the Vizier? I want to go home."

Out of nowhere, Sabu appeared, his green

eyes glowing. "The Vizier? Why, he went back to Thebes."

"He couldn't." I struggled up. "Not without me."

"He had to report the tomb robbery," Sabu said.

I stared at him, unable to believe it. "But the Vizier will be in trouble if he comes back without Pharaoh's Cat."

"Oh, he took a cat with him," Sabu said. "One that looked just like you, in fact. A friend of mine. I think he's looking forward to palace life. Neferhotep the goldsmith even put your collar on him."

"What?!" An imposter had stolen my place?

"Looks like you're stuck here in Set Ma'at," Sabu said cheerfully.

I fainted dead away.

CHAPTER 10

Stranded

When I came to, Khepri was bouncing across my face.

"Ra?" He prodded at my cheek with his foreleg. "Ra, are you all right?"

"How can I be all right?" I moaned. "I've been replaced by another cat! And I've been banished to this lousy, no-good excuse for a village—"

"Shhh!" Miu flicked her ears in warning.

I blinked and saw Sabu standing behind her. Judging from his offended glance, he'd heard every word.

I tried to claw my way back. "I mean, I'm sure it's fine if you grew up here—"

"It's way better than a flashy palace,"

Sabu growled. "Call yourself a cat! Real cats don't sleep on gold-embroidered pillows."

I rolled to my feet. "Hey! I don't sleep on gold-embroidered pillows. Gold thread is *much* too prickly—"

"That's enough." Miu put herself between us. "Both of you, behave."

"But I've just lost my home forever." I'd never make it through the desert to Thebes on my own, even if the Nile weren't in the way. "And I've lost my necklace from Pharaoh. And my *snacks*. My scrumptious, one-of-a-kind, made-just-for-me *snacks*."

"Very sad," Miu said. "But you'll live. And it won't be forever, Ra."

"That's right," Khepri chimed in. "Pharaoh won't be fooled, Ra. He won't accept a substitute cat. He'll send the Vizier right back for you."

"You really think so?" I said.

Sabu gave a cat-shrug, but Miu brushed against me in a comforting way. "Of course, Ra," she said. "The Vizier's sure to come back. Maybe not right away. But soon."

Khepri settled himself against my ear.

"After all, there's no other cat like you, not in the whole of Egypt."

"True." I cheered up. "Pharaoh can't do without me. Not for long, anyway." At least I hoped so.

"And really, when you think about it, we're *lucky* to be stranded here," Khepri went on. "Now we have a chance to crack the case."

Lucky? I wouldn't go that far. But he had a point.

"We'd better get down to business, then," I said. "The Vizier could be back at any moment, and when he comes, I'm out of here. So we need to solve this case."

"What case?" Sabu asked. "What are you talking about?"

"It's a secret," I told him.

"No, it's not," Miu said. Ignoring my protests, she laid out everything we'd discovered. "So it's someone in this village," she finished. "We just don't know who. We could use your help."

Sabu tilted his head curiously. "You mean, you're trying to *solve* this case? Why not leave it to the humans?"

"We can't," Miu said. "They haven't noticed any of the clues."

"But we're Great Detectives," Khepri piped up with pride. "We notice everything."

"Great Detective?" Sabu swished his tail, a sign of interest. "That sounds like a job that would suit me."

"We have enough detectives already," I said. When Miu glared at me, I added reluctantly, "But if you really want to help, I guess you could be our sidekick."

Sabu looked like he couldn't believe what he'd just heard. "I'm not anybody's sidekick, Fancypaws. I'm a leader. Go find some other cat to help you."

Head held high, he stalked off.

Fancypaws again! The nerve. But when I turned to Miu to complain, she said, "Ra, stop making trouble. We need him on our side. He's the leader here. I bet there's not a cat in Set Ma'at who will talk to us without his say-so."

Hmmm . . . I hadn't thought of that.

Miu was still watching Sabu's angry tail. "We'd better go after him before he disappears completely. But this time, Ra, let me do the talking."

"Good idea," Khepri agreed.

By the time we caught up with Sabu, Bek was hand-feeding him snacks again. Honestly, the way that cat could eat! And did he offer to share? No.

As we came into view, he turned his face away and butted his head against Bek's knee.

"The Scribe says nobody's allowed in the Valley of the Kings until the Vizier returns," Bek was saying to Sabu. "So we can't work on Pharaoh's tomb today. But that means I get to see more of you—"

"Bek." A stocky man hustled up to the sculptor. "We need to talk."

It was Neferhotep the goldsmith, the man who had given my necklace away. *Oh, little beads that go clink!* I put my claws out.

"That sculpture you were going to make for my tomb? I want it bigger." Neferhotep stretched his restless hands apart, showing the size he wanted. His rings sparkled in the sharp sunlight. "Twice as big, in fact."

Bek gave Sabu one last stroke, then straightened to his full height. "Are you sure, Neferhotep? It will take longer, and it will cost three times as much."

"Don't be ridiculous." Neferhotep jabbed a ringed finger at Bek's chest. "Twice as much, that's all I'm paying you."

"That wouldn't cover the costs," Bek explained patiently. "A bigger stone is much more expensive—and that's before I even start carving it. But maybe there's some other compromise we can come to. Come to my place, and we'll discuss it."

As he and Neferhotep walked away, I saw the boy Kenamon slip out of an alley and follow them. I pointed him out to Khepri.

"Maybe he's going home," Khepri offered.

"Or maybe he's trying to get a closer look at those rings on Neferhotep's fingers," I countered. "I swear he has more now than he did when we got here. Maybe one of them comes from Setnakht's tomb."

"If it does, he'd be pretty silly to wear it where everyone can see it," Khepri said. "You're getting carried away, Ra. Yes, Neferhotep gave your necklace to another cat. But that doesn't mean he's a criminal."

"Sure it does," I grumbled. "He stole my necklace, for starters."

I sat down in the shade, and Khepri slid between my paws. Behind us, Miu trotted up to Sabu.

"Cousin, I'm so sorry!" She spoke in her sweetest purr. "Ra was just teasing. He knows you're a born leader. We all do. How could anyone doubt it? You're clearly in charge here in Set Ma'at, and we need your help." She bowed her head to him. "Please, cousin, will you be our partner?"

Sabu looked torn. Cousinship is a strong tie among us cats. Even seventh cousinship, twice removed.

"Look," he said to Miu. "I want to help

96

you. But I won't take orders from that high-hat palace cat, and that's final."

Well, he wouldn't be working for us, then.

But Miu continued in that sweet purr, "You don't have to take orders from him, cousin. You and I can work together. I could help you organize the village cats into a detective force. You'd be so good at that!"

Sabu lapped up her praise. "You're right. I'd be great." His gaze flickered back to me. "Maybe I could give *him* orders."

"All right. That's enough." I hauled myself to my feet. "Nobody gives orders to Pharaoh's Cat. Khepri and I will pursue our own investigations, thank you very much."

"We will?" Khepri said.

I gave him a look. "Yes, we will."

"We can meet up and compare notes later," Miu said, trying to keep the peace.

"Yes." There was laughter in Sabu's green eyes. "Then we'll discover who's the *real* Great Detective."

CHAPTER 11

Filthy Beast

It was all I could do to get out of there without starting a cat fight. But Pharaoh's Cat knows how to behave with dignity. With Khepri perched on my head, I padded my way down the narrow main street of Set Ma'at.

When I was sure we were out of Sabu's sight, I came to a halt.

"Did you hear that?" I fumed to Khepri. "Sabu's turned this into a contest. He thinks he's a better detective than I am."

"That's not necessarily a bad thing," Khepri said, "if it means he works hard."

"Great Detective, my paw! Why, he couldn't handle being a sidekick." I was still fuming. "I'll show him. I'll crack this case before the Vizier comes back for me—with time to spare."

"We'll crack it together," Khepri said. "Where do we start? With Neferhotep?"

"No." I didn't even have to think twice. "We'll get to him later. But we'll start at the top." What better place could there be for Pharaoh's Cat? "We're going to interview the highest-ranking animal in Set Ma'at."

"You mean Sabu?" Khepri said doubtfully.

"Of course not." I scowled. "Sabu can brag all he wants to, but we know who the real top animal is."

"Who?"

Wasn't it obvious? "Well, it's the Scribe who's head of the village. So the top animal is his favorite pet. He had the boy Kenamon paint her portrait. Remember? What's-her-name."

"Menwi?" Khepri said.

"Yes, that's the one."

"What sort of animal do you think she is?" Khepri wondered.

"Something classy, no doubt, with a name like that." The original Menwi had been a great lady in the royal court. "I'm guessing she's a cat of fine lineage. Or perhaps a monkey or a falcon."

Khepri looked down the street of tightly packed houses. "And where do you think she lives?"

"Oh, that's easy. We'll look for the biggest place in the village. Only the best will do for the Scribe."

Khepri thought this over. "So he'll have the best snacks, too?"

Khepri is quite clever sometimes. "Another reason to always start at the top, my friend."

In the end, we identified the Scribe's front door by smell alone. As the village boss, he had the fanciest midday meal.

"This is it, Khepri." The aroma of cumin and duck made my head swim. It wouldn't count as anything special at the palace, but I was too hungry to care.

I bounded toward the steps just as the Scribe himself came along, accompanied by Huya, the strapping young carpenter. They appeared to be in deep discussion, keeping their voices low, but when the Scribe saw me, he broke off. "Shoo!"

"I'm Pharaoh's Cat," I meowed indignantly. Not that it did any good.

"Go on, shoo!" The Scribe brandished his inky staff at me, narrowly missing my tail. I yowled.

"My lord, stop! That's Pharaoh's Cat." Kenamon rushed up to my side.

Relieved to have a defender, I turned back to the Scribe. *So there!*

"Don't be ridiculous, boy," the Scribe sneered. "Pharaoh's Cat went back with the Vizier."

"But this is the one I was drawing, my lord. I'm sure of it. He's even got a beetle on his head—"

"And probably bugs all over the rest of him, too," the Scribe interrupted. "He's a stray, boy. Look at him."

"But—"

"Don't waste my time, Kenamon. I've had enough trouble from you and your family today. Can't you see Huya and I have important matters to attend to?" The Scribe turned to his brawny companion. "Huya,

wait out here, and I'll bring you, er . . ." He
flashed a glance at Kenamon and lowered
his voice. "Well, just wait here," he went on
to Huya. "And don't let that filthy beast in.
I don't want him mucking up the place and
bothering Menwi."

"Yes, my lord Scribe." Huya elbowed
Kenamon out of the way and planted himself in front of me.

"Who does the Scribe think he is, calling me filthy?" I protested to Khepri. "He's the one with the inky fingers."

"Yes," Khepri said uncertainly. "But . . ."

"But what?"

"Well, the trip out to the tomb didn't do you any favors, Ra. I hate to say it, but you're not quite the same cat."

For the first time since we'd gotten back, I took a close look at myself. My hind end was covered with dust. My tail was matted. My paws were mottled with clay. And those were just the bits I could see.

"This isn't good." A chill went through me. "Even if the Vizier does come back, he'll never recognize me."

"Of course he will," Khepri said, a shade too heartily. "We need to clean you up, that's all."

As the Scribe vanished into his house, Huya aimed a kick right at my hindquarters. "Scoot, you dirty stray!"

I scooted before I was booted.

Kenamon followed after me, and when we reached a safe place, he bent down and held a hand out. He didn't seem to mind how dirty I was. "Sorry, Pharaoh's Cat. The Scribe shouldn't have done that to you, and neither should Huya. But they're awful to almost everybody. In fact, I think they might be up to—"

"Kenamon, who are you talking to?" Pentu the painter rounded the corner. His hands had flecks of rusty paint on them, and his gaunt face was winched tight with worry. "Oh, it's just a cat."

Kenamon stood, his feet arranged as if to guard me. "It's Pharaoh's Cat, Father."

"Pharaoh's Cat?" Pentu didn't look past my dusty fur. "You have quite an imagination, Kenamon."

"He got left behind somehow," Kenamon insisted. "He needs water and food."

"Kenamon, you know we can't afford to feed a cat. Not even Pharaoh's Cat. Which I doubt this is."

"But I thought you said that things were going to change—"

Pentu looked alarmed again. "Hush."

Some cat wisdom: when people say "hush," it's time to listen up. I swiveled my ears, determined to catch every word of what came next.

CHAPTER 12

Secrets and Surprises

"We're not going to talk about that again."
Pentu's voice was hardly more than a whisper. "Do you understand?"

"I don't see why we have to keep so quiet about everything," Kenamon mumbled.

"Silence is golden."

"But you spoke out this morning. Loud and clear, right to the Vizier."

"And look at the trouble that caused." Pentu sighed. "Kenamon, you need to leave that cat alone and come with me. Neferhotep wants to see you about painting one of the walls of his tomb."

Neferhotep again? I bared my teeth as I saw the goldsmith approach us.

Kenamon looked at his father in surprise.

"I thought you said he couldn't afford our prices."

Neferhotep overheard. He knotted his fingers together as he stopped in front of Kenamon. "Your father and I have come to an arrangement."

"An arrangement?" Kenamon looked uncertainly at his father. "What are the terms?"

Pentu didn't meet his eyes.

"Never mind," said Neferhotep. His fingers were twitching again, so rapidly that I could hear a constant clinking as his rings tapped against each other. I sidled closer, trying to get a good look at those rings. Did one of them belong to Setnakht? "The point is that your father and I have agreed that you will paint a portrait of me on the wall of my tomb. Come with me, and I'll tell you exactly what I want."

He turned and motioned for Kenamon and his father to join him. As Pentu followed, a narrow reed brush dropped from his waistband.

Scooping it up, Kenamon sighed, then bent low and whispered to me. "I have to go with them, but wait here. I'll bring you some water as soon as I can. And a snack, if I can find one."

He ran off, leaving me alone with Khepri.

"Did you catch that?" Khepri asked.

"About the snacks? Of course." I never miss anything about snacks.

"Not that, Ra. Did you hear how Pentu told Kenamon they were going to have more money soon? He even said that he's not supposed to talk about it. And he's clearly done some kind of funny deal with Neferhotep. Looks suspicious, doesn't it?"

"Not really," I said, but I was uneasy. "You can't possibly suspect that nice boy of being a criminal."

"It was the father I was wondering about," Khepri said. "Maybe Neferhotep knows he's the tomb robber, and he's blackmailing him. Though maybe the boy is involved, too. He did behave rather strangely in the tomb. He was watching us so closely, and he seemed to notice everything, but—"

"He's an artist," I said. "He's *supposed* to notice things. That doesn't make him guilty. And remember, he offered me *snacks*."

Khepri dropped down onto my nose,

looking cross. "Snacks don't mean anything, Ra."

I stared at him aghast. "Khepri, snacks mean *everything*."

Khepri sighed and climbed back between my ears. "I suppose we can't really build a solid case against anyone until we have more evidence."

"Well, after Kenamon brings me my snack, we can go look for more clues," I said.

"Kenamon only said he'd *try* to come back. It doesn't mean he will. Anyway, we can't just sit around and wait for Kenamon. We're Great Detectives, and we've got a case to pursue."

He was right. But that didn't mean I had to be happy about it.

"So where were we?" Khepri drummed his feet on my fur. "Oh, yes. You wanted to go interview Menwi, the Scribe's pet. And I agree that might be useful. I vote we try the Scribe's back door."

Pharaoh's Cat doesn't normally *do* back doors, but Great Detectives can't afford to be fussy. With Khepri guiding me, I darted down alleys and squeezed through gaps until we reached a small courtyard behind the Scribe's house.

"See that shed?" Khepri murmured as we balanced on the wall. "Maybe Menwi lives there."

"In a shed off the kitchen? Be serious, Khepri. No highborn cat—"

The Scribe bounded out the back door, a pot in his hand. "Menwi, darling, it's lunchtime!"

With grunts and squeals, an enormous pinky-white mountain rushed out of the shed. A mountain with a curly tail and a snout.

I looked at Khepri in shock. "Menwi is a *pig*?"

"The biggest pig I ever saw," said Khepri in awe.

"But everyone knows that swine are allied with the forces of chaos," I said. "No one keeps them as pets."

"The Scribe does," Khepri said. "Just listen to him!"

"Who's the cleverest creature in Egypt?" The Scribe blew a kiss to Menwi. "That's right. It's you, darling." He dumped the

Menwi

contents of his pot into a trough. "Spiced goose for you, my sweet. And some other goodies."

"Spiced *goose*?" Khepri whispered in my ear. "What do you want to bet the spices are cinnamon and cumin?"

My thoughts exactly.

Menwi snuffled at the trough.

The Scribe scratched behind her ears. "I wish I could stay, beloved, but I need to keep one step ahead of the Vizier." He blew her more kisses as he left. "See you soon, my darling."

"He blows kisses to a pig, but he won't let Pharaoh's Cat into the house?" I couldn't get over the injustice. "That's it. I'm going home."

Then I remembered I didn't have a home. Some other cat had taken my place. All I had was this.

Khepri hopped off my head, the better to observe the pig. "I think we should talk to her, Ra. If she really is the cleverest creature in Egypt, she might be able to help us."

"She doesn't look that smart to me," I said.

"She's certainly worked out how to get plenty of food," Khepri noted.

Point taken.

"All right," I said. "We'll talk to her."

"Good. You know, I really like how it smells here—"

"But we're not staying long," I added.

"Then let's get going." Khepri meant to hop up on me, but in his excitement, he overshot. When I reached out to catch him, we both went tumbling down into the courtyard.

We landed in something soft.

And smelly.

And squishy.

"Dung!" Khepri cried in delight.

"Dung!" I cried in horror.

I jumped up, reeking, and found myself muzzle-to-snout with Menwi.

CHAPTER 13

Menwi

"Goodness gracious, what have we here?" Menwi had the accent of a highborn lady— well-bred, cultured, and just the faintest bit amused.

Bedraggled and stinky though I was, I pulled together what dignity I had left, assuming the time-honored pose of Bastet. "Lady Menwi, may I introduce myself? Pharaoh's Cat, Ra the Mighty, Lord of the Powerful Paw, at your service."

(I didn't mean the "at your service" bit. It's just what we aristocrats say.)

Menwi's beady eyes looked me up and down. "Well, whoever you are, you certainly do sound like royalty. I've never seen a cat with such elegant bearing—or so covered with mud. Why, you could almost be a royal piglet."

Khepri sprang to my side. "Oh, he's Pharaoh's Cat all right. He's just having a bad day."

"The worst ever," I confided. "I've had to crawl through tombs and walk through deserts. I've had jackals chasing me and people kicking me. And I haven't had a thing to eat since I left the palace."

"You're hungry?" Menwi looked horrified. "Why, that's dreadful." She swung her snout toward her trough. "There's not much left, but you're very welcome to it. And . . . er . . . your companion as well."

"Thanks," Khepri said cheerily, "but I've already eaten."

"I'm not even going to think about that," I told him. Nodding politely to Menwi, I said, "I'm honored, but I wouldn't dream of taking a lady's food."

"How polite." Menwi regarded me with approval. "But really, it's more than I can manage. The Scribe is so generous. It's there for the taking, if you change your mind."

"No, no," I murmured. "You're too kind." I didn't want to offend her, not when we were trying to get on her good side, but I wasn't about to lower myself by eating a pig's leftovers. I sidled past the trough. If there was any spiced goose in there, I couldn't tell, given what a reeking jumble it was.

Wait a minute. Was there *duck* in that mess?

Hmmm, I thought. *I do love a bit of roast duck.*

"Well, maybe I will have just a taste . . ." I plunged my head into the trough.

A big mistake. There was roast duck, all right—well past its prime. But it was mixed with moldy melon and rancid gravy. And now that gravy was clinging to my fur.

Choking, I retreated to Menwi's water dish.

"Such a dainty appetite," Menwi said in concern. "Are you sure you've had enough?"

"Urgggh . . . yes. Thank you." I hacked up a bit of duck and batted it away with my paw, hoping she wouldn't see.

"Well, now that you've eaten, do please tell me more about yourself, Ra the Mighty.

What brings a royal cat like you to Set Ma'at?"

"I'm here to serve justice," I told her.

"We both are," Khepri put in.

Together we told Menwi about the tomb robbery.

"So the thieves come from this village?" With a squelch, Menwi lowered herself to the ground next to me. "It's shocking that Set Ma'at would be involved in something so disgraceful. But I can't deny that standards have slipped here. And now tomb robbery . . . well! It just shows what this world is coming to."

"So you'd be willing to help us?" I said.

She opened her pale lashes wide. "Of course."

"Then tell me everything you know against Neferhotep," I said.

"Ra," Khepri warned, "that's not the way a Great Detective solves—"

"Neferhotep the goldsmith?" Menwi interrupted. "He's a thief if there ever was one."

"A thief!" I repeated. "Did you hear that, Khepri?"

"Why, he charged the Scribe an absolute fortune for repairing the clasp of a gold collar," Menwi went on. "And when the Scribe refused to pay anything but a reasonable fee, Neferhotep said he would get the money out of the Scribe one way or another. He sounded quite threatening." She tutted. "I'm afraid he's not a nice man at all. He actually said"—she lowered her voice—"that I *smelled*. I've heard he has connections with a gang of some sort, too."

"Does he?" I said, excited. "A gang of tomb robbers, maybe?"

Menwi's small eyes gleamed. "Quite possibly."

"Hmmm." Khepri sounded less enthusiastic. "Could I ask if you have any actual evidence, Lady Menwi? Maybe you saw Neferhotep sneaking out of the village last night?"

"Oh, goodness me, nothing like that," Menwi said. "I never pay much attention to the comings and goings of common workers. And I'm always in bed at a reasonable hour." With a delicate snort, she added, "A lady needs her beauty sleep, you know."

"Of course," said Khepri gallantly, but I could see he was disappointed. So was I. There was nothing to prove Neferhotep's guilt.

"The trouble is, that leaves the field wide open," Khepri explained to Menwi. "Anyone from Set Ma'at could have been the robber." He began pacing around Menwi's water trough. "All we know for sure is that someone got into Setnakht's tomb through the stonework in Thutmose the Second's abandoned tomb next door. There's no other way in. And we know it was someone from the village because of the clues we found there."

"The spiced goose," I murmured wisely.

"So I guess that means it's most likely to be a tomb worker," Khepri went on to Menwi, "since they could have explored the place during their breaks."

"No, they couldn't," Menwi contradicted him. "The Scribe is careful about that. He has the guards watch the workers very closely. They're accompanied everywhere— on the path up to the tombs, inside the tombs, everywhere in that whole area. The men aren't allowed to take breaks alone, and they're searched every time they leave the building site. Then they're searched again before they come home to Set Ma'at."

I nodded. This much I knew. "It's a high-security operation, Khepri."

"If they're watched so closely, then how did anyone discover the way into Setnakht's tomb?" Khepri wondered. "Because somebody did discover it. We know that for a fact."

"What about the thieves who robbed Thutmose the Second's tomb a few years ago?" I suggested. "Maybe they found the way in—and came back for more."

"No," Menwi said slowly, her curly tail spiraling. "That robbery happened two years ago, and I remember the Scribe telling me about it. The thieves were caught that night, with the loot still in their bags, and they only had treasures from Thutmose the Second's tomb. Nothing else. Besides, they were executed."

"Not much chance of them being involved, then," Khepri murmured.

"What if Anubis brought them back from

the dead?" My whiskers trembled as the full force of the idea hit me. "Don't you see? It fits. Dead tomb robbers could slip through anywhere—"

"Don't be silly, Ra," Khepri said. "The tomb was robbed by living people. The scraps we found were fresh, remember? And I'm sure those blocks had been moved." He sighed. "We just don't know who did it. I'm afraid we're stuck."

"Not quite," Menwi said.

CHAPTER 14

A Charming Model

"Not quite?" Khepri repeated.

"Well, the robbers weren't the only ones who went into Thutmose the Second's tomb," Menwi explained. "The Scribe told me there was a hole in the roof where the thieves got in, so they couldn't seal it up again. It had to be abandoned. But even though the robbers had tried to burn it to cinders, there were a few bits and pieces that survived the fire. So the Scribe sent a handful of men to retrieve what they could. And since we don't have extra guards to spare, I suppose it's possible they weren't watched as closely as usual."

"Aha!" I was getting excited again. "Who were the men on the clearance crew?"

Menwi wriggled her snout, as if to jog her memory. "Let me see. The Scribe told me he sent Huya the carpenter and Neferhotep the goldsmith, because there wasn't much work for them that day on the site. Oh, and Pentu the painter was there, too."

Kenamon's father? I didn't like the sound of that.

"And were there any others?" I asked, hoping there were.

One ear flopped over her eye. "No one else."

"What about the Scribe?" Khepri asked. "Didn't he have to go to Thutmose the Second's tomb to check on the work? He could have found the way into Setnakht's tomb then."

Menwi stiffened. "Are you implying that my Scribe is a *criminal*?"

"No," said Khepri, "I was just—"

"Because if I thought that you were," Menwi continued, "you would get no further help from me." She snorted in indignation. "In fact, I'm inclined to think that this interview is over."

Khepri was watching her with a funny look in his eyes. "Really? I think perhaps you—"

"Shhh!" I hushed him.

He went on. "—protest too—"

What else could I do? I put my paw on him. Very gently.

"—much," he finished, but my fur muffled the word.

"My dear lady," I said to Menwi as Khepri spluttered, "it is refreshing in this day and age to see such loyalty. But I'm sure my friend Khepri here was merely wondering if perhaps the Scribe might have seen some valuable clues."

Soothed back into good nature, Menwi said, "No, everything was in good order. There was no reason to suspect any of them of wrongdoing. But if you ask me, I'd look very carefully at Neferhotep. Did I mention that his uncle was a tomb robber?"

Another strike against Neferhotep.

"Is he close to his uncle?" Khepri asked.

"Not anymore. His uncle was executed a long time ago," Menwi said. "Maybe ten years back? But that kind of thing does tend to run in the family, you know. Of course, Huya may bear watching, too. He's been getting too big for his boots lately, and his brother is the Captain of the Guard. Perhaps they're working together." She stifled a yawn. "But you must excuse me now. It's time for my afternoon nap."

A nap sounded good to me. As Menwi trotted daintily toward her shed, it was all I could do not to roll over and fall asleep myself.

Khepri, however, was wide awake. "We need to get to the bottom of this story about Neferhotep's uncle, Ra. And learn more about Huya and the Captain of the Guard." He wriggled up my fur. "Come on! Let's investigate."

"All right, all right." I leaped back up to the wall. "But I bet I'd be more efficient if I just had a quick doze."

"You want to sleep?" Khepri chirped in dismay. "Ra, we're in the middle of an important case."

"It wouldn't take long." I skimmed my way along a wall that connected the backs of several houses. "Look at that courtyard there, Khepri. The one with the awning. Talk about a perfect spot for napping."

"No, Ra."

I jumped down. "But see, it's so quiet. And it even has a charming model of a temple and tomb—"

"Dirty kitty!" A small child shrieked behind me. "Dirty kitty!"

I darted to the left, but it was too late. A whole pack of tiny humans had surrounded me.

I've spent enough time with Pharaoh's children to know what would happen next. Sure enough, the boldest one grabbed me by the middle. It was what he said afterward that surprised me.

"Let's bury the cat in the tomb!"

Pharaoh's Cat never bites children, but I was tempted.

"Put me down!" I meowed. "Right now!"

The child lifted up the top of the model tomb and dropped me inside, Khepri still clinging to my head.

"And now we seal the tomb!" the boy shouted.

The top of the tomb clunked down.

We were trapped.

CHAPTER 15

Trapped in a Tomb

"Open up!" I meowed to the children. "Immediately!"

Khepri was crawling the walls. "They're not listening to you, Ra. I don't think they can even hear you. This model's made out of stone."

"Then I'll just have to meow louder." I gave it all I had. "Enough is enough, children! This is Pharaoh's Cat speaking. Get me out of here."

Khepri clicked in my ear.

"And the beetle, too!" I added.

Nothing happened, except I noticed how dark it was. And how quiet.

"I think maybe they've gone away," Khepri said.

I stretched, trying to dislodge the lid of

the tomb, but it wouldn't budge. Same with the walls.

"It's solid," Khepri said. "I think we're stuck."

"Great." I slumped down on the tiled floor. "How long will the air last?"

"I don't know," Khepri said, "but I guess we'll be okay for a while."

"You *guess*? Khepri, this is a matter of life and death. A guess isn't good enough."

"It's all I've got," he chirped. "Anyway, look on the bright side: you can get that nap you wanted."

"How can I nap, knowing I'm about to suffocate?" I started to feel woozy just thinking about it. I wafted the precious air with my tail. "Is it me, or is it getting hard to breathe in here?"

"If you can't nap, then let's discuss the case," Khepri said.

"Khepri, I'm dying! And you want to talk details?"

"Great Detectives never let themselves get distracted," Khepri said. "Now, I know Menwi didn't want to talk about the Scribe visiting the abandoned tomb—"

"Don't talk to me about tombs," I warned him. "I can only handle one at a time."

"Ra, be sensible—"

"I *am* being sensible," I wailed. "If you're trapped in a tomb, it makes sense to panic!"

"Ra, please calm down."

"What if we die here, Khepri? What if Anubis comes to weigh our souls?"

All of a sudden the top of the tomb flew off, and something plunged down toward us.

"It's Anubis!" I shrieked. "Beware the gods!"

But it wasn't a god reaching for us. It was Kenamon.

"Ra the Mighty? I'm so sorry." The boy lifted me out and set me gently on the ground, Khepri gripping my tail. "My little sister told me what happened, and I came to rescue you."

His little sister had put me into that tomb?

"She didn't mean any harm," Kenamon went on, "and she wasn't the one who dropped you in there, but I've told her and the others that they're never to treat a cat like that again. Especially not you."

He turned, and I noticed that there was a small girl standing behind him. Like most little kids, she wasn't wearing anything at all, and her head was shaved except for one long sidelock of hair—but she had the same alert, worried eyes that Kenamon and his father had.

"It's okay, Isesu." Kenamon put a reassuring arm around his sister. To me, he said, "She is awfully sorry."

She should be, I thought. But Isesu looked so sad that I softened. She wasn't much older than Pharaoh's own youngest daughter, who was hardly more than a baby. Besides, she had told Kenamon everything—and that was what had saved me. I guessed I could forgive her.

Eyes brightening, Isesu reached for me. "I want that kitty."

I jumped back. Forgiveness only goes so far.

"He's not yours," Kenamon said firmly. "He belongs to Pharaoh."

Isesu pouted. "But I want him."

"Maybe someday we'll have a cat," Kenamon told her. "A different one. Not this one."

"Someday when we're *rich*," the girl said happily. "Are we rich now, Kenamon?"

"Hush." Kenamon pulled his sister closer to him. "Father doesn't want us talking about money."

Isesu wrenched herself free. "Then let's play!"

"In a minute." Kenamon set a cup down before me, with a tiny portion of what smelled an awful lot like spiced goose. "It's all I could take from my meal without Father noticing," he explained to me. "But it's yours, if you want it. And there's water in the trough against the wall."

"Kenamon? Isesu?" Pentu called to them from inside the house, and then his anxious face appeared at the door. "Where are you?"

"Here we are!" Isesu ran toward the door.

"I have to go," Kenamon murmured.

As he dashed away, I snarfed up the goose stew in one bite. Sure enough, I tasted cinnamon—and a touch of cumin.

"Hey!" Miu appeared at the top of the wall at the end of the courtyard. She jumped down to us. "I see you found a snack, Ra."

"Miu!" I was glad to see her, but then Old Green Eyes appeared at the top of the wall.

"Oh," I said, with less enthusiasm, "I see your cousin's with you."

"We've made an incredible breakthrough." Miu was so excited that even her ragged ear had perked up. "It turns out Sabu is really good at this detecting business." She motioned for us to follow her. "Come on. We have a lot to tell you."

"I'm not so sure I want to talk," I mumbled as Khepri climbed onto me. But I went ahead and followed Miu over to the next house, where Sabu had staked out a spot by a palm tree.

"Well, look at what the dung beetle dragged in," he drawled as I approached. Then he caught a whiff of me. "Whew-*ee*. Is that some more of your fancy palace perfume? Smells like pig."

"Hush, Sabu," Miu said. "Tell them what we've discovered."

"Thanks to my army of cat informants," Sabu said, "we've narrowed the field of suspects—"

"So have we," I announced. "We're down

to Huya the carpenter and Neferhotep the goldsmith and the Scribe of the Tomb."

"And Pentu the painter," Khepri finished, jumping down between my paws. "He's a possibility, too."

"But not a likely one," I told Miu. "Did you know Neferhotep's uncle was a tomb robber?"

"That doesn't mean Neferhotep is one, too," Khepri said to me.

"But it's more likely," I said.

Khepri disagreed. "I don't see why—"

"This is how you guys play detective?" Sabu gave us a cool flick of his ears. "You make wild accusations and argue about them?"

"They're not wild accusations." I set him straight. "And we don't 'play detective.' We *are* detectives. Great ones. That's how we found this stuff out."

I let Khepri give them the details of our interview with Menwi.

Sabu looked taken aback.

"So much for wild accusations," I said. Pharaoh's Cat might be covered in mud, but he was hard to beat.

"Wow," said Miu. "You found out a lot."

"It's easy when you're a Great Detective," I said. "So what did you two discover?"

"Plenty," said Sabu, with just the edge of a snarl.

Miu quelled him with her paw. "We started from the other end, working out who was where on the night of the robbery. Luckily, we had Sabu here to organize the village cats for us. He did an amazing job."

The compliment seemed to soothe Sabu. "It was a matter of leadership. I told them there had to be two witnesses for each alibi, and they had to report back to me."

"Take Sabu's human, Bek, for example," Miu told us. "Sabu was one witness to the fact that Bek was home last night, and the goose next door was the second. She says Bek's snoring kept her goslings awake all night."

"We cats were having a party ourselves last night," Sabu said. "So that made things more complicated. But a smart leader always gets the job done."

"We've narrowed the field to a few suspects, and they're the same as yours," Miu said. "Pentu the painter, Huya the carpenter, Neferhotep the goldsmith, and the Scribe of the Tomb. They all contributed spiced goose to the feast, and none of them have strong alibis for later that night."

It was an impressive piece of work. Maybe Sabu was worthy of being our sidekick.

But then he said something to Miu that got me in a cat-twist. "You forgot to mention Kenamon, Pentu's son. He doesn't have an alibi, either."

"Oh, come on, Sabu," I said. "He's too young to be a tomb robber."

"If he's old enough to work in the tombs, then he's old enough to rob them," Sabu said. "Besides, he could have been helping his father."

"Talk about wild accusations," I said.

Sabu twitched his ears in annoyance. "I just told you. The boy's father is a suspect, and the boy himself doesn't have an alibi. That's not an accusation. It's a fact. And there's more."

"More?" I didn't like the sound of that.

Was I wrong about Kenamon and his father?

CHAPTER 16

Suspicions

I looked down at my paws as Sabu outlined the case against Pentu and Kenamon.

"Everyone here knows that Pentu's family needs money to pay off their debts," Sabu said, "and Miu's told me about the strange way Kenamon behaved in the cave. Plus, one of my cats heard the boy and his father arguing this morning. She didn't catch everything, but it was about keeping something a secret."

Uh-oh. I felt a prickle of worry. "Probably just some family tiff," I said to the others. "Let's not make too much of it."

Sabu narrowed his green eyes, but it was Miu who spoke first. "Ra, you have to admit there's a case to be made against Pentu—and maybe against Kenamon, too.

But everybody should remember that we have other suspects as well: Neferhotep, Huya, and the Scribe." She turned to her cousin. "Sabu, what do you know about the Scribe?"

"Well, there's no question he went into Thutmose the Second's tomb, whatever Menwi says," Sabu told us. "It's his job to investigate tomb robberies and file a report. Though whether he filed an honest report is another question."

That got Khepri's attention. "So the Scribe isn't trustworthy?"

"I've heard he takes bribes sometimes," Sabu said. "And people say he and the Vizier are as thick as thieves."

"That's just an expression," Khepri protested.

"Maybe not," Miu said. "I mean, look at the way they're running this investigation. The Scribe and the Vizier aren't exactly knocking themselves out to crack the case. They didn't want to open the tomb, and they swallowed the whole Anubis story without question. They're not even trying to find other explanations."

"Good point!" Khepri tapped the ground, as if he were thinking things through.

Not that anything needed thinking through. It was perfectly obvious what had happened.

"They formed a conspiracy," I told the others. "They realized it would be easier for two people to rob the tomb. Especially if one of them was in charge of the guards."

"Although I think one person could do it," Khepri put in, "if he was strong enough. Those blocks were pretty loose."

"No, they're in it together," I said. "That's what my instincts tell me."

"I'm not sure I'd go that far," Miu said. "We don't have any evidence—"

I swished my tail. Evidence could come later. "I always said that Vizier was up to no good, didn't I, Khepri?"

"I thought you just didn't like him," Khepri said.

"I had my reasons, Khepri. Honestly, a man who treats cats like that is a menace. And the Scribe is no better. But we have them in our sights now. They won't escape us."

"*If* they're guilty," Khepri put in. "We have other suspects, you know. Weren't you the one saying it was Neferhotep who was guilty?"

"I didn't commit myself," I said. "Now that I've had time to consider the facts, I think it's the Scribe and the Vizier."

"Well, I'm not committing myself to anything," Khepri said. "Not until we have more evidence." He thought for a moment. "Sabu, did your cats notice anything else last night? Someone climbing the village wall, for instance? Or walking around where they weren't supposed to be?"

"No," Sabu said. "We asked, but no one saw anything unusual."

"It doesn't help that lots of them were having their own parties last night," Miu added. "Or that we had that sandstorm before dawn. It wiped out all the smells, so sniffing around didn't tell us anything, either."

"Too bad." Khepri clicked in disappointment. "Well, what about the treasure? The thief must have hidden it somewhere. Let's look for that."

"I've already ordered my cats to search for it." Sabu sounded very superior. "I told them to make Pentu's place a priority, but he keeps chasing us away. Suspicious, don't you think?"

"Well, the Scribe wouldn't let me into his house, either," I said. "I'd say that's suspicious, too."

"Not when a cat is as dirty as you are," Sabu said.

I bristled. "Is it any wonder I'm dirty? This whole village is a mess."

"Are you criticizing my home?" Sabu's back arched, and his fur went spiky. "I've had enough of your insults, you little palace fusspot—"

"How dare you speak to Pharaoh's Cat like that?" I said, outraged.

Miu darted between us, and Khepri hopped after her, which I'll admit was brave of him, since he's teeny-tiny and Sabu and I were both making ourselves look as scary as possible.

"Cut it out, you two," Miu ordered.

"She's right," Khepri agreed. "We need to work as a team."

Sabu and I slowly stepped back from each other.

"Sabu, how about we go see how the search is going?" Miu said, coming up beside him. "Ra and Khepri, you can come along, too, and meet some of the cats."

Meet Sabu's gang? "No thanks," I said as Sabu rose to go with Miu. "We've got our own leads to pursue."

"We do?" said Khepri.

"We do," I said to him. "Hold on tight."

But when I hopped over the wall, a fierce gray beast careened toward us.

"Jackal!" I shrieked. Khepri flattened himself in the fur between my ears.

But I was wrong. It wasn't a jackal. It was something even worse: Boo, the guard dog.

Sleek and eager, he raced up to me, licking his muzzle with his big pink tongue. "Hi there, Pharaoh's Cat! I'm free now. Want to play?"

CHAPTER 17

Run Around

"Um . . . no," I said to Boo. "No playing for me today."

"Not even one game of tag?" Boo said, his dark eyes hopeful.

Tag? With a guard dog? *I don't think so.*

"Sorry," I said. "I'm on duty. You know how it is."

Boo scratched his head in confusion. "Wait a minute. Pharaoh's Cat has a *job*?"

"He's a Great Detective," Khepri piped up from between my ears. "And so am I. That's why we were asking you all those questions earlier, remember?"

"About the clues and the tombs and all?" Boo nodded. "Sure, I remember that. I didn't realize it was a full-time job."

"It is," I assured him. "A *very* full-time job. Not a minute to myself. No time to play. Ever."

"Aw, that's too bad." Boo bobbed his head in sympathy. "When the Captain of the Guard brought me down here to Set Ma'at, I thought for sure that we'd have time for a game."

"What's the Captain doing here?" Khepri asked.

Boo scratched his head again. "I don't know exactly. He doesn't usually come into the village. But I think he wanted to see his brother Huya. Actually, the Captain seems upset with him. I heard them arguing."

"What about?" I said, suddenly alert. Huya was one of our suspects.

"Who knows?" Boo said. "Though I think I heard the Captain say something about gold."

"Gold?" Even Khepri was excited by that.

"But maybe he said *cold*," Boo mused. "I wasn't listening closely. It was kind of boring, really. That's why I came to find you instead. It made me so happy when you started that game this morning. Nobody wants to play with me anymore, ever since that little accident last year." He looked at me hopefully again. "You sure you can't play? Just for a bit?"

"Nope," I said swiftly. "I'm on a case."

"Oh, go on and play with your friend, Ra," a voice called. I looked up and saw Sabu sitting on the wall, a big cat grin on his face. How long had he been there?

"Hi, Sabu!" Boo greeted him eagerly. "How are things? Want to play?"

"I'm on a case," Sabu told him. "The same one as Ra."

Boo regarded him with respect. "So you're a Great Detective, too?"

"The Greatest," Sabu assured him.

"Why, you haven't solved a single mystery, you great big boaster," I spluttered.

But Sabu was still speaking to Boo. "And since I'm on the case, we can spare Ra. You two run along, and have a good time together."

"Really?" Boo's eyes shone. "That's great." As Sabu disappeared over the wall, he turned to me, paws clicking. "Did you hear that, Ra? I'll give you a head start, and then I'm coming after you!"

"*Yeooooooooowl!*" I shot forward like

one of Pharaoh's spears. "Sabu, I'll get you for this!"

I darted straight up the same wall where he'd disappeared, but I couldn't see him anywhere.

"Hey!" Boo scrabbled at the bottom of the wall. "No fair going up where I can't reach you."

"Boo?" The Captain of the Guard strode down the alley, brows twisted in a frown. I thought again how much he looked like Huya. "Here, boy! Let's go."

Boo sighed but obeyed. "Sorry," he called back to me. "Guess I'll catch you later."

"Not if I can help it," I murmured, flopping down on the top of the wall. But it wasn't really Boo I was mad at. He was just doing what dogs do. Sabu, on the other hand . . .

"Khepri, can you believe the nerve of that cat? Calling himself the Greatest Detective, and then siccing Boo on me?"

"That wasn't very nice," Khepri agreed, hopping down onto the wall beside me. "But frankly, you haven't been nice to him, either."

"Why should I be?" I scraped my claws

against the stones. "He's called me Fancy-paws and fusspot—"

"And you insulted his village. Remember: we need his help."

"He started it," I grumbled. "That loud-mouth alley cat."

Khepri gave me a long, hard look. (Perhaps you've never seen a beetle's eyes close up. Trust me, they can bore right into you.) "Ra, why are you quarreling with Sabu over everything? Why can't you be more gracious? You're Pharaoh's Cat, but you're acting like a stray fighting over scraps."

Ouch! Even my old buddy was starting to think of me as a stray.

Shaken, I looked down at myself, and what I saw wasn't reassuring. I was dirtier than ever, as slovenly a cat as I'd ever seen. I didn't look fit for the alleys of Set Ma'at, to say nothing of Pharaoh's shining palace.

And if Khepri was right, the changes hadn't stopped there. Was I losing my royal grace?

Well, that settled it. Forget the nap. I needed to prove I was truly a royal cat. But if Khepri thought I was going to do that by being nice to Sabu, he could think again.

I had another plan, a much better one: What I needed to do now was solve this case. Then I'd be a hero and the greatest Great Detective, and everyone would know I was Pharaoh's Cat. Sabu would be put in his place, once and for all.

There was just one problem. I looked down at my unkempt paws.

Where did I start?

"I think I need a snack," I said faintly.

"Later, Ra." Balanced on the edge of the wall, Khepri was peering down the alley. "Look! Neferhotep's coming this way."

So he was. He crossed paths with Huya, who turned to glare at him and then stomped off in the other direction.

"We need to investigate those rings," Khepri said as Neferhotep came closer.

"His rings . . . ?"

"You said he had too many," Khepri reminded me. "You thought one of them might come from Setnakht's tomb. This is our chance to look. Who knows? He could be wearing Setnakht's heart scarab under his tunic."

Neferhotep did have a lot of jewelry. You could hear him jingling as he came our way. He was singing, too—a ditty that sounded like "I'm a lucky, lucky man . . ."

Maybe it was the singing, but I started to feel woozy. "I can't investigate on an empty stomach, Khepri."

"Then I'll do it!" With a valiant cry, Khepri launched himself onto Neferhotep's bald head.

CHAPTER 18

Slap!

The moment Khepri touched him, Neferhotep shrieked. His jewelry jangled, and his hands went stiff.

"Khepri, watch out!" I shouted.

Slap! Neferhotep struck his head where Khepri had landed.

Luckily, he only hit himself. Khepri was already on his shoulder.

"Get off me, you creepy thing!" Neferhotep screamed.

Slap! Slap! Neferhotep's blows came fast and hard. But Khepri was even faster. He wriggled down to Neferhotep's chest, then scrambled under his tunic.

Neferhotep yelped and grabbed a sharp stone from the ground.

"Jump, Khepri!" I yelled. "He'll smash you to bits."

"Not . . . done . . . yet . . ." Khepri popped out at Neferhotep's wrist, clinging on for dear life.

As Neferhotep tried to scrape him off with the stone, I leaped into action—and I do mean *leaped*. I landed on Neferhotep's shoulders and wrapped myself around him like a fur collar.

"Help!" Neferhotep dropped the stone and clutched at his chest. "Get away from me, you vile beasts!"

"I'll vile *you*," I muttered, but Khepri had dropped to the ground, so I did, too. "Climb aboard, buddy."

Once Khepri had a good hold on my fur, I bounded back up the wall out of reach. Fearing Neferhotep might pick up another stone, I kept moving down the wall. But when I glanced back, he was being comforted by Bek, who had come running to his aid.

"A cat and a bug attacked you?" Bek was saying. He sounded puzzled. "Are you sure? I have to say, it doesn't sound like something a cat would do. They're lovely creatures, cats—"

"Not this one." Neferhotep shuddered. "He's a real beast, I tell you. And he smelled disgusting. Like something that had died." He scuttled away down the alley, looking thoroughly spooked. Bek followed, shaking his head.

Like something that had died?

I sniffed myself delicately. Okay, so I smelled a bit stronger than usual. But that was no reason to be rude.

"Tell me he's guilty," I said to Khepri.

"I didn't see the heart scarab," Khepri said, "or anything else that looked like it belonged to a pharaoh. But maybe I missed it." He sounded dazed. "Everything happened so fast."

Well, that was a setback. "Maybe he's got the loot hidden at home. That would be a smarter place to put it."

"Or maybe he's innocent," Khepri said. "We just don't know, Ra."

I stopped padding down the wall. "I do know one thing."

"What's that?" Khepri asked.

"I need a snack *now*."

"Hey!" Khepri surged up into my fur. "Let's go investigate the house next door."

"But I'm hungry," I protested.

"You can't be, Ra. You just had that snack from Kenamon. And you ate from Menwi's trough, too."

"Don't remind me." My ears flattened just thinking about it. "I'm never eating leftovers again—"

"Ra, if you don't move soon, he's going to get away."

"Who?"

"Huya the carpenter. I saw him on the roof terrace next door. I think that's his house. He's just gone downstairs."

"You think he's hiding something? Like treasure?"

"It could be," Khepri said. "But we'll never know if we don't get moving."

"Right." It was hard to ignore that hungry feeling inside, but the life of a Great Detective requires some sacrifice. "Hold on, Khepri!"

In three bounds, I was over the wall. I landed in the dusty patch of ground behind Huya's house—only to find myself face-to-face with an angry goose and her goslings.

"Out! Out! OUT!" the goose honked. "Out this minute, or I'll report you to Sabu next door. He promised my goslings would be safe, and he'd better not go back on his word—"

"We won't do you any harm." Khepri popped out from behind my right ear. "We just have a few questions."

At the sight of him, the goslings let out excited peeps.

"Mom, it's a beetle!"

The Goose and Goslings

"Yum!"

"Can we eat him?"

"He can be your afternoon snack, my dears," the goose honked, "if he and his friend don't get going."

"Yikes!" Khepri burrowed into my fur. "Ra, get me out of here."

CHAPTER 19

Silly Goose

"Don't worry," I whispered to Khepri. "I know how to deal with geese. You just have to show them who's boss."

As Khepri cowered behind my right ear, I jumped to the top of what must have been the goose house and proclaimed in my most regal tones, "I am Ra the Mighty, Pharaoh's Cat, and this beetle is under my royal protection. We are Great Detectives, and you must cooperate with our investigation."

"Do you think I'm a fool?" The goose snapped her orange bill. "Look at you! Pharaoh's Cat, indeed. You're nothing more than a jumped-up alley cat. I'll report you to Sabu, I will."

I scrabbled to keep my grip on the goose

house. "Fine. Go to Sabu, if you want. He'll confirm it: I'm the Lord of the Powerful Paw." Or would he just call me Lord Fancy-paws?

The goose was close enough to see the doubt in my eyes. "A likely story."

I dug my claws into the goose house. "It's the truth, you silly goose!"

"*Silly goose?*" Her neck pumped. A bad sign.

"A figure of speech," I said hastily, but it was too late.

She flapped her clipped wings, rising just high enough to reach me. "Get OUT!" Her golden beak flashed, aiming straight for my tail.

"*Raaaaaaa!*" Khepri wailed.

I sprang up onto the nearest wall.

By now, the goose was making such a clatter that everyone in the house was peering out—including Huya, who was frowning, instead of smirking. So much for any chance of sneaking up on him.

But Pharaoh's Cat isn't one to give up easily. "Look," I called down to the goose, "I'm fighting for justice here—"

Huya charged out of his house. Those bulging muscles of his weren't just for show. He moved as fast as an arrow, and he had a heavy hammer in his hand. He looked even angrier than he had when he'd crossed paths with Neferhotep. "Scat!"

An energetic woman jumped out from behind Huya's shadow and jabbed at me with a broom. "You leave our geese alone, you stinking stray!"

Yikes! That broom had a long reach. I needed a brushing—but not like that. I darted into the next yard.

"Whew!" Khepri croaked in my ear. "Ra, next time you want to show somebody who's boss, remind me not to be there."

"I got you out, didn't I?"

"At the last possible second," Khepri mumbled. "I never want to be that close to a goose again."

Truth was, neither did I. Putting some more distance between me and that beak, I trotted along the boundary walls. "Khepri, tell me the truth. Do I really stink?"

"Oh, no," Khepri said. "You smell great."

The more I thought about it, the less

reassuring that was. "You mean I smell like—"

"Ra, look over there," Khepri interrupted. "Kenamon's up to something."

"Kenamon?" Turning, I caught a glimpse of the boy darting into a niche between two houses, then snaking his way up a section of back wall that was largely screened off from view. He was moving like a cat—a cat who didn't want to be seen.

Part of me had to admire him. The rest of me was worried. A boy who could move like that wouldn't just make a good cat. He would make a good thief.

Was I wrong? Was Kenamon guilty after all?

"Let's follow him," Khepri murmured.

I made a beeline for the boy, cutting through the courtyard next door and leaping up to the wall. If I could get the boy to sit still long enough, maybe I could pry the truth out of him with my purr. As I've mentioned, that's the one bit of real magic cats have. Of course, it works best with people you're strongly attached to, but I felt a bond with Kenamon, so it was worth a try.

"Faster!" Khepri said in alarm. "He's getting away!"

The boy was slipping away as quietly as he had come. I was about to spring after him when Khepri cried out in terror. "Ra!"

I didn't so much see the brick as hear it, whistling down to crush me.

CHAPTER 20

Nefru

"What was that?" I said groggily.

"Hold on, Ra." Khepri's chirp wasn't as cheerful as usual. "Miu's coming."

I saw two of her dashing toward me, then blinked and saw one.

"What happened?" She crouched beside me, worried. "I've been looking for you everywhere. I didn't expect to find you sprawled half dead in Pentu's courtyard."

Pentu's courtyard? Was that where I was? I blinked and caught sight of the model tomb. Not the most comforting sight, frankly.

"He's lucky he's not all the way dead," Khepri said. "A brick fell and nearly killed us."

"I jumped," I muttered. It was coming back to me. "Just in time."

"But then the brick shattered on the wall, and some of the pieces hit you," Khepri told me.

That explained the ache in my tail. I stretched out my paws and wriggled, determined to get back on my feet. "It's not so bad. Nothing broken."

Miu sighed. "Honestly, Ra, you attract trouble."

"I think this time trouble was aiming at him," Khepri said.

"Did someone throw that brick at me?" I drew myself up. *Ouch.*

"These houses are well built," Khepri said. "Bricks don't fall from well-built houses. Besides, what are the odds that a brick would knock you over just as we were chasing Kenamon—"

"Well, the boy couldn't have done it," I said. "He was over there." I waved in the general direction with my tail. *Double ouch.*

"But maybe someone in his family did," Khepri argued. "His father owns this house, and I think the brick came from their balcony."

"Probably an accident," I said, but my voice was faint.

"Or maybe the boy led you into danger," Khepri said.

"Let's move you to Sabu's yard," Miu urged. "Sabu's out looking for the treasure with his cats, but he won't mind. It's right next door, and you'll be safe there."

Sabu's yard wasn't my idea of a place to recuperate, but Miu wouldn't take no for an answer.

"Hey," Khepri said as we scrabbled down into the tiny yard. "Sabu *is* here. Wait, no— it's just a kitten."

So it was: a small tabby maybe three months old, curled up by a half-carved statue. When she saw us coming, she started to back away.

"Don't go," Miu called out. "We're friends of Sabu's."

The kitten hesitated. "Do you know where he is? I need to talk to him."

"He's on the other side of the village, investigating a tomb robbery," Miu said kindly. "Can we help?"

"That's what I need to talk to him about."

The kitten trembled. "The robbery."

"Well, you can talk to me," Miu told her. "I'm his cousin. And this is Pharaoh's Cat, and—"

"Pharaoh's Cat?" The kitten looked at me in wonder. "Really? I thought you left."

"I didn't," I said, a touch grimly.

She frowned. "But you don't look like Pharaoh's Cat. You're so dirty, and your fur's messed up, and you smell like—"

"I'm working undercover," I said, my voice even grimmer. When she ducked her head, I added more peaceably, "What's your name, young one?"

"I'm Nefru," she said softly. "I belong to the household of Neferhotep, the goldsmith."

"You do?" I gave the others a significant glance. "And what is it you want to tell Sabu?"

"I saw Anubis," Nefru said.

Khepri gave a disbelieving click.

"You what?" I stared at the kitten.

"I saw Anubis," Nefru repeated. "Last night. He climbed over the village wall in the middle of the night."

— NEFRU —

"Why didn't you tell us this before?" Miu asked.

"Nobody told me what was going on," Nefru said. "I'm just a kitten, you see. And I didn't tell anyone else, because I was too scared. But then I overheard what the other cats were saying, and I thought I'd better find Sabu."

"How did you know it was Anubis you saw?" I asked.

"He had a jackal's head and a human's body," Nefru said, as if explaining the obvious. "Nobody else looks like that. And he wasn't a dream. He was just as real as can be."

Her clear gaze made my fur prickle. She was too young a kitten to deliberately lie. "Maybe Anubis really is behind the tomb robbery," I murmured to Miu and Khepri.

"Don't be ridiculous." Khepri's reedy voice floated down from the top of my head. "It must have been somebody in disguise. Nefru, did you see where he came over the wall?"

"At the end of Pentu the painter's court-yard," Nefru said.

Miu and Khepri exchanged a glance, and

I knew what they were thinking. *Another piece of evidence against Pentu.*

"Maybe you're remembering it wrong," I suggested to Nefru.

She looked up at me, wide-eyed. "No, I'm not. He came over the wall right where Pentu lives. I saw it."

"It's easy to get confused about these things," I told her. "Especially at night. Tell me, is there any chance this Anubis looked like someone you know? Like, say, Neferhotep?"

"Of course not," she said hotly. "Neferhotep doesn't look like Anubis at all. Not one bit."

My whole body was aching, but I stayed patient. "Are you sure? Neferhotep doesn't have an alibi—"

"I knew I should have waited for Sabu." The kitten pulled back from me. "He would have understood."

"Look, kid," I told her. "I outrank Sabu—"

She bolted.

"Oh, dear," Miu said. "You shouldn't have spoken to her like that, Ra. She won't confide in any of us now."

"Miu's right, Ra." Khepri hopped down from my head. "You blew it."

I was fed up. "Fine. You want this case solved, you do it yourselves. You two and the oh-so-wonderful Sabu." I dragged my weary body over to a far corner of the courtyard. "I need a nap."

Out of my half-closed eyes, I saw Khepri and Miu whisper in concern and then tip-toe away.

They'll never get anywhere without me, I thought to myself.

Yawning, I stretched out in my patch of sunlight. I might be muddy and disheveled and missing my golden collar, but I was willing to bet I was still the best catnapper in Egypt.

Take forty winks, I told myself. *Forty winks to dream about all the snacks you're missing back at the palace.*

Tender chunks of antelope smothered in gravy . . .

Grilled duck wings with cardamom sauce . . .

An entire ox turned on the spit . . .

My forty winks became eighty, then doubled again.

The sun was low in the sky when Khepri came back and tugged at my ear.

"Wake up, Ra! We've caught the thief!"

CHAPTER 21

Guilty

I sat bolt upright. They'd caught the thief without me?

"Actually, it was the humans who caught him," Khepri said, scrambling up my fur. He led me down three houses to the Scribe's grand residence.

"So it was the Scribe?" I said. "I knew it!"

"No," Khepri said sadly. "Not the Scribe. Pentu the painter. Kenamon's father."

"Pentu?" I was horrified. Entering the courtyard, I saw the painter surrounded by the Scribe and four hulking servants. Pentu's paint-speckled hands were bound behind his back, the rope twisted so tight that it hurt to look at it.

"I swear I didn't do it," Pentu gasped. "I

have no idea how that earring got into my paint box—"

"Liar!" The Scribe struck the painter's head with an inky hand. "Thief! Did that son of yours help you? Where is he?"

"I don't know." Pentu's voice was broken. "But he's innocent, I swear it."

"Then why has he gone missing?" The Scribe hit Pentu again, harder this time. "And where is the treasure? We've searched your house and grounds. Where did you hide it?"

"I told you, I didn't steal—"

This time the Scribe slammed into Pentu with his staff. As the painter sagged from the blow, the Scribe leaned in close, his voice full of menace. "We'll break you, Pentu. There will be nothing left of you by the time we hand you over to Pharaoh." Turning to the servants, he said, "Lock him up in the cellar. I'll deal with him once we find the boy."

"I'm innocent, and so is Kenamon!" Pentu cried as they dragged him away. That earned him another blow to the head.

I felt sick. Awful as it had been to see Pamiu's mummy on the floor, this was far worse. At least Pamiu had been dead a long time. Pentu was alive. What would the Scribe do to him? And what would happen to Kenamon and his little sister?

Miu slipped from the shadows with Sabu.

Sabu threw me a triumphant glance. "What did I tell you? It was Pentu who did it."

"They've got the wrong man," I told him.

"Don't be ridiculous." Sabu preened his whiskers. "I was there. I saw it all. I *predicted* it. And that makes me the real Great Detective."

"In your dreams," I said.

Sabu laughed. "No, in yours. You were the one sleeping on the job."

I was starting to regret that nap.

"What exactly did you see, Sabu?" Khepri asked. "I know Pentu, Huya, and Neferhotep were redecorating a room for the Scribe's wife, but I didn't hear what happened."

"Pentu's paint box slipped to the ground," Sabu said. "No surprises there. He's always dropping things. But a gold earring fell out, and that got everyone's attention. The Scribe read the tiny hieroglyphs on it, and it comes from Setnakht's tomb. So he had Pentu arrested."

Even to me, it sounded like an open-and-shut case. Luckily, Pharaoh's Cat is very, very good at opening what's shut—whether that's the door to the banquet hall, or a case that looks hopeless.

"Someone planted the earring," I suggested. "I bet it was the Scribe. After all, it happened in his house."

"It could have been Huya," Khepri said. "Or Neferhotep. They were right there, too."

"No," Sabu said. "I saw their faces when the earring fell out. They were surprised."

"Maybe they're just good actors," I mumbled, but I was getting worried. This was a strong case against Pentu.

"Admit it," Sabu said to me. "I was right. I'm the Great Detective."

"So where's the treasure?" I shot back. "You can't be a Great Detective if you only solve half the case."

Sabu twitched his ears in annoyance. "The treasure is with the boy. Isn't that obvious?"

"You'll never convince me," I said.

Sabu rolled his eyes. "You liked the attention Kenamon gave you, I get that. But you're a fool if you can't see that he ran off with the loot."

I glared at him. "I don't know about you, but I don't make wild accusations—"

"So where is the treasure, then?" Sabu said. "My cats have been combing this village for hours. If the loot from the tomb were here, they would've found it."

"Maybe the treasure was never stored in the village in the first place," Khepri said with a pensive click. "I suppose it's possible Kenamon ran away with it—"

"Just like I said," Sabu put in.

"Khepri!" I squinted upward, trying to catch a glimpse of him, but it's impossible to see between your own ears. "You're on *my* team, remember? Not Sabu's."

"That's one possibility," Khepri continued. "Another possibility is that the thief hid the treasure somewhere outside the village."

"Great." Sabu sat down heavily on his haunches. "Now you expect my cats to investigate every nook and cranny in the hills?"

"What if we start with what's closest?" Miu suggested. "We could explore the cliffs near the village, where the villagers' tombs are."

I remembered Boo mentioning the workers' tombs, but I hadn't been paying much attention then. I was paying attention now.

"One of the cats was telling me about them," Miu went on. "They tend to be small, and they aren't guarded like the pharaohs' tombs. They might be a good place to hide something."

Sabu considered this. "Maybe you're

right, cousin. But my cats are exhausted, and I can't ask them to do anything more today. Besides, it's almost sunset, and they think the tombs are creepy. We'll go tomorrow instead."

Tomorrow sounded good to me, too— until I thought of Pentu in that dark cellar, and his missing son.

I stretched out my sore body and tried not to moan. "No. We go now."

"Don't be stupid," Sabu said. "You don't want to get caught in the desert at night. The jackals will hunt you down."

Yikes! I'd forgotten about the jackals.

"We'll go first thing in the morning, okay?" Sabu yawned and swerved his rear end right in my face. "And now, if you don't mind, I need to get some rest. Unlike some other cats I could mention, I haven't been napping all day. Miu, if you come with me, I've got an extra mat I could lend you."

As he headed off, Miu looked at me apologetically. "I don't want to take the only mat—"

"Don't let me stop you," I said huffily. "I wouldn't sleep near Sabu if you gave me an entire roast ox." *Though maybe two . . .*

I guess I was too huffy, because Miu trotted off without another word.

Khepri slid down my head a little. "Ra, we'd better look for a place to bed down, too. It'll get dark quickly once the sun sets."

"How can you talk about sleep at a time like this?" I asked him.

"Er . . . I thought you liked sleeping, Ra."

"I do," I admitted. "But this is our moment, Khepri."

"Our moment for what?" Khepri inquired cautiously.

"Cracking the case! While Sabu's sleeping, we'll dash out to the workers' tombs—"

"Past the jackals?" Khepri asked, alarmed.

I'd been alarmed, too, when Sabu had first mentioned them. But after he stuck his rear end in my face, I'd reconsidered.

"He's just trying to scare us off," I told Khepri. "He knows he won't be a Great Detective unless he finds the treasure, so he doesn't want us to get there first. But if we go now, we'll be the ones who find the treasure and solve the crime." I couldn't help adding, "And I bet you anything that it wasn't Kenamon."

Khepri mulled this over. "Well, I'd like it if we were the ones to solve the mystery. And I really hope that Kenamon isn't guilty. But I'm still worried about the jackals."

"Miu said the tombs are close to the village," I reminded him. "We'll be there and back before you know it."

"Not if the jackals catch up with us, Ra."

"They won't," I said. "And if they do, they won't bother us. I showed them who was boss earlier."

"That's not how I remember it," Khepri mumbled into my ear.

"Trust me, Khepri. We Great Detectives have to stick together. Now hold on tight."

Before Khepri could raise more objections, I marched out the village gate, headed to the tombs.

CHAPTER 22

The Breath of Anubis

As I trotted out to the villagers' tombs, the golden sun was almost touching the tops of the western cliffs. There was no sign of the jackals, but my long shadow crept behind me like a snake on the desert sands.

Khepri twisted against my ear, and I guessed he was looking back toward the village. "Let's hope the Vizier doesn't come looking for you now."

"If he does, he'll just have to wait," I said. There was no way I was going to let Sabu steal the title of Great Detective from me. Not when I was this close to claiming it back.

The sands were cooling off now that the heat of the day had passed, but I was weary as we neared the miniature pyramids and temples of the village tombs. I came to a stop by the first open doorway I saw.

"This one belongs to the Scribe," Khepri said. "See his name up there?"

"You can read?" I said in amazement.

"A little," Khepri said modestly. "I'm learning."

"Well, if this place belongs to the Scribe, we're searching it top to bottom," I said as we entered.

As it turned out, there wasn't much to check.

"Call this a tomb," I sniffed, gazing at the cramped walls. "Why, Pharaoh's wig box is better decorated. And they're only just digging out the burial chamber."

"That's probably because the Scribe has to spend all his time working on Pharaoh's tomb," Khepri said. "Not to mention yours."

I didn't know what to say to that. I wanted a gorgeous tomb, of course. But until now I hadn't considered what that meant for everyone else.

"Well, anyway," I said, "I don't think we're going to find any treasure here." And we didn't, not even in the rubble.

After that, we went into a tomb that was even more lackluster than the Scribe's. Honestly, it was hardly big enough for a single sarcophagus, let alone the food and furniture and clay servants that a person needed in the afterlife. It did have one glory, though—a wall of remarkable paintings.

"That's Kenamon's father," I said, stopping in front of one of them. "And it's Kenamon who painted him. I can tell."

"This must be their family tomb," Khepri said.

Because it was so small, it didn't take long to investigate, and there was absolutely nothing in it.

"Not a single speck of gold," I said with satisfaction.

"Let's hope that's not because Kenamon's hidden it somewhere else," Khepri said.

"He hasn't," I insisted. "You'll see. Where's Huya's tomb?"

We located it quickly: the tomb with the most elaborate carpentry—including an intricate wooden ceiling.

"Maybe it has secret panels," Khepri said. "I sure wish we could find a way up there."

"No problem," I told him. "Cats are the best climbers."

Which was sort of true. But they can't walk upside down, so I had to give up.

"We'll come back," I promised.

After we saw a potter's tomb and a stonecutter's tomb, we stumbled across Neferhotep's tomb, which wasn't much more than a load of bricks and the start of a hole in the ground.

"I don't think the treasure's here," Khepri said.

Neither did I, so we moved on to the next tomb, which was more substantial: an empty space half carved out of the rock, with a ledge and some rough columns at one end of it, and at the other, a familiar figure . . .

My eyes widened in the dim light. "Sabu?"

He remained eerily still.

"What are you doing here?" I asked.

He said nothing, and I began to get scared. Was it Sabu's father? Or maybe . . . his ghost?

Behind me, I heard a faint meow, as if

from a feline spirit. Shivering, I backed away, but Khepri crept forward until he was right under the cat's nose.

The cat didn't move a whisker.

It *was* a ghost!

Now Khepri was crawling onto the ghost's paw.

"Khepri, leave that ghost alone!" I hissed.

Khepri giggled. "It's not a ghost, Ra. It's a statue of Sabu. This must be Bek's tomb."

"Oh." Relieved, I came forward to inspect the statue. "It's a very good likeness—"

"*Meoooooow!*"

There it was again, that cat cry, only louder this time.

I went still. "Now, *that* sounded like a ghost."

"It sounded like a cat to me," Khepri said.

"A cat ghost," I clarified as Khepri hopped back onto me. I was getting worried again. "One of Sabu's ancestors, maybe. Or—"

"There you are!" Miu bounded in.

"Miu?" I was startled to see her. "What are you doing here?"

"I couldn't get to sleep, so I went for a

walk, and I saw you in the distance, crossing the desert." She glanced around the lonely tomb. "What were you thinking, coming out here by yourselves?"

"We're looking for the treasure," Khepri told her excitedly.

"And we're not going to stop now," I said.

"But it's almost dark," Miu pointed out. "The sun's setting."

I peered at the doorway behind her. Now that she mentioned it, the sky was looking distinctly less bright than it had a few minutes ago. But if I gave up, then Sabu would win.

"Great Detectives don't care about the dark." I leaped up onto the shadowy ledge. "They keep going wherever the case takes them."

As I started to sniff around, Miu jumped up to the ledge, too. The shadows were so deep that I could barely see her, but her voice was impossible to miss. "Ra, I'm serious. You don't want to be stuck out here after dark. Sabu's told me how dangerous those jackals can be. And there's something else that worries me. When I was climbing up here, I saw Huya on the cliffs above you—"

"Huya?" Khepri cut in. "What's he doing out here?"

"I don't know," Miu said, "but I hope he didn't see me. I didn't like the desperate look on his face. And I think I saw a jackal hiding behind a rock—"

A chill went down my spine.

Khepri felt me shiver. "What's wrong, Ra?"

"The breath of Anubis," I whispered. "I can feel it on my fur."

"Anubis?" Khepri chuckled. "Don't be silly, Ra."

"I tell you, I can." The sun must have set, because the tomb was almost completely dark now. "There's something wrong here."

"It's fine, Ra," Miu said from the other end of the ledge. "Calm down."

A chill went over me again. The whole place was growing spookier by the moment.

"There's someone in here," I said, with growing conviction. "Someone in the dark with us—"

"Stop it," Khepri whispered. "You're scaring me now."

"I'm scared, too," I whispered back. "I tell you, Anubis is here—"

"Ra, please," said Miu.

"He's *here*," I told her. "He's lying in wait for us!"

In the darkness, I heard something rustle.

"*Aaaaaaaaaaaah!*" I bolted out of the tomb.

"Ra, come back!" Miu chased after me.

Above me, Khepri's scream was like a tiny whistle. "*Raaaaaaaaaaaaaa!* The jackals are out here!"

I'd forgotten. But in the twilight, I saw their glowing eyes just below us.

"*Anoooooooooooooooooobis!*"

The jackal gang had found us.

CHAPTER 23

The Jackals of Anubis

Before we could duck back into the tomb, the jackals cut our way off. Within moments, they had us hemmed against the cliffs.

"We're trapped!" Khepri cried.

"Beware the jackals of *Anooooooooobis!*" The whole gang took up the cry. At noon, they had laughed at us, but there was no laughter now. Only menace. *"Anoo-oooooooooooobis!"*

The leader stepped forward, wolfish teeth gleaming in the moonlight. "I warned yooooooooooooooou," he howled. "I told you to stay away from the tooooooooooombs!"

"Up here, Ra." Miu flashed past me, leading the way to a tiny gap in the rocks. With Khepri clutching the top of my head, I flew in after her, just in time to avoid becoming a jackal's dinner.

"I hope you're satisfied," Miu said, once we were settled.

"Um . . . sort of." The new quarters were extremely cramped, much more so than the last tomb. But that wasn't so bad. "At least there's no space for anyone to lurk in the dark with us."

"Shhh!" Khepri warned. "If we talk, those jackals will stay close by. We want them to give up and go away."

We were silent for a long while, listening to the howling outside our hidey-hole.

"Beware, introoooooooooooooooooders! The jackals of *Anoooooooooooooooooooobis* will have their revenge!"

Eventually, worn out, I dozed off, only to wake up with a start, my heart pounding.

"Who's there?" I called out.

"Only Miu and me." Khepri crept back over to me. "We were talking."

"I thought we weren't supposed to talk," I said.

"That was ages ago," Khepri said. "It's

past midnight, I think. And the jackals have backed away, at least for now."

"Well, I'm not taking any chances," I said. "I'm staying until daylight."

"I think that's wise," Miu agreed. "Though I wish we could investigate that last tomb again. Ra, what made you think someone was in there with us?"

"Didn't you hear the rustling? Couldn't you feel his breath?" Remembering made me shiver again. "I tell you, Anubis was there. And he called the jackals to him."

Outside, a faraway jackal howled, as if in echo. *"Anooooooooooooooooooobis!"*

I shuddered.

"That's what you keep saying, but I don't believe it," Miu said flatly. "If there was someone in there, I bet it was Huya. Or maybe Kenamon."

"Why would they be hiding in a tomb?" Khepri wanted to know.

"Maybe they were retreating from the jackals," Miu said.

"But why would they be up here on the cliffs in the first place?" Khepri wondered.

"Because they're guilty, and they're trying to avoid the authorities," Miu said. "Or maybe because they think the treasure's somewhere up on these cliffs. Somewhere we haven't looked yet."

"There certainly are a lot of hiding places up here," Khepri mused. "These cliffs are riddled with holes and gaps."

"Kenamon's innocent," I reminded them. "I'm sure of it."

Miu hardly seemed to hear me. "Maybe Huya blackmailed Kenamon into helping him."

"Or maybe Huya robbed the tomb by himself," I countered. "Or maybe he's co-operating with the Scribe and the Vizier. I thought we agreed it was fishy that they didn't want to investigate inside the tomb."

"There are endless possibilities," Khepri said, sounding discouraged. "Sometimes I think humans are too complicated—"

"I don't think the thing in the tomb with us was a human," I said unhappily. "I tell you, I felt the breath of Anubis on my fur."

"Oh, Ra." Miu nudged me with her paw. "Don't start that again."

"I did. I really did. It's the creepiest

thing that's ever happened to me." I sank my head onto my paws, looking for some kind of comfort. "I wish I was back home at the palace."

"No point thinking about that now," Khepri said.

"I can't help it," I moaned. "What if we never get back there? What if the jackals get us first? What if *Anubis* does?"

"Ra, please." Miu nudged me with her paw again. "Let's talk about something else."

"The case," Khepri suggested. "Let's talk about the case."

"Why?" I wailed in despair. "We'll never crack it. Not if the gods are involved."

"It's not the gods," Miu insisted. "And I'm sure we can solve this case. If worse comes to worst, we can just follow the money."

I sat up, bewildered. "What are you talking about?"

"Whoever has all that loot is rich, Ra," Miu explained. "Eventually he'll give himself away because he's spending too much money."

"There's not a lot of money in Set Ma'at,

so he'll stand out," Khepri added. "If somebody buys precious jewels, or starts making his tomb or his house extra fancy—"

"Huya's tomb is fancy," I said, remembering that intricate ceiling. "And so is the Scribe's house. And Neferhotep was going to buy a tomb portrait from Kenamon, remember? He ordered an extra-big statue from Bek, too."

"True," Khepri said. "And Kenamon hushed his little sister when she asked if they were rich now. So I guess it could be any of them."

"It wasn't Kenamon," I muttered.

"It sounds like none of them makes much money," Khepri went on, "so I can see why they'd be tempted to steal from a tomb."

"You know, I thought the tomb workers would be paid better," Miu said. "It's sad to see so many families struggling to get by."

"When you think of the beautiful art they make for Pharaoh, it seems like they deserve more," Khepri agreed.

"Yes." Miu sighed. "I'm not saying it's right to rob a tomb. But how can it be right to bury all that gold when people need it?"

I shuffled my paws uneasily in the darkness. I wanted a beautiful tomb. But I agreed that the people of Set Ma'at deserved better—especially Kenamon.

"People get so worked up about their tombs," Miu went on. "I just don't understand it. If you ask me, what matters is how we treat others in this life. That's the true memorial, and that's what will count when Anubis weighs our souls. Not some golden rooms in the side of a cliff."

"*Anooooooooooooooooooooooooobis!*" The howls outside were growing louder. "*Anooooooooooooooooooobis!*"

A muzzle snuffled at the gap in the stone.

"They're trying to get in," I yelped, drawing back.

"They're too big to fit," Miu said. "I think." But she retreated, too.

I squirmed into a fold in the rock and burrowed as deep as I could. Some of the rock crumbled, letting me worm my way farther back.

Khepri let out a strange click.

"Hey, buddy," I said. "Are you all right?"

"I'm okay," he said. "But there's something odd about this rock."

As he spoke, the rock gave way beneath me, and we tumbled down in a flurry of stones.

CHAPTER 24

Gold Everywhere

Before we even hit the ground, Miu was calling to us. "Ra? Khepri?"

"I'm fine," I croaked, shaking myself free of pebbles and debris. "What about you, Khepri?"

"I'm okay," he chirped from somewhere to the right of me. "But I don't know where we are."

"Me neither." I trained my ears and nose on the darkness around me. "From the echo, it sounds like a big place. And it smells musty. I'm talking really, really *old*. And sort of . . . spicy." I stopped sniffing as the horrible truth dawned. "Khepri, I think we're in a *tomb*."

"I'm coming to help!" Miu called.

"Miu, don't," I warned.

Too late. She landed next to me. "Wow. That's a big drop," she said as a few pebbles bounced down after her. "How are we going to get up to the cave again?"

"That was my point," I said hollowly. "Now we're all trapped—in an ancient tomb."

"We'll find a way out," Khepri said confidently.

"We're doomed," I moaned. "Doomed, I tell you. No one will ever find us, and we'll waste away in the darkness . . ."

Except it wasn't so dark anymore. A faint light was glowing somewhere to our left.

Khepri scuttled toward it. "Hey, watch out," he warned us. "There's a big hole here. I mean *really* big."

A hole? I stopped moaning and squinted. Khepri was right. On our left there was an enormous hole, right at the mouth of a tunnel. The light seemed to be coming from the far end of the tunnel.

"Maybe it's a pit to trap tomb robbers?" Miu trotted forward. "Yes, look at that. Those are some serious spikes at the bottom. And look, someone's laid some rope across the pit—"

Khepri scrambled forward for a closer look. "It's a rope bridge."

The faint light wavered and grew brighter.

"Someone's coming," Khepri said, hopping back to me.

"Anubis!" Strangled by fear, I could barely whisper the warning. "He lured us here. It's been his plan all along. He's coming!"

"Not Anubis *again*," Miu said, but I saw apprehension in her eyes as the light grew stronger.

"Hide!" I choked out. "Quick!"

Turning back, we could see the chamber we'd fallen into. It was indeed a tomb, with a polished stone sarcophagus and ghostly statues covered with jewels and gold. On the floor was a heap of still more jewels—including an enormous amethyst heart scarab. There was a small golden sarcophagus set carefully beside it . . .

A *cat-shaped* sarcophagus.

I twitched my whiskers in shock. The loot from the tomb robbery!

The light grew brighter, and then I saw

him, coming down the narrow tunnel toward us . . . *Anubis*.

His black jackal head was enormous, the body beneath it veiled like a priest. When he reached the pit and the rope bridge, his robes billowed out, and he seemed to fly across it. Quaking, I ducked behind the nearest statue with Miu and Khepri.

"I told you Anubis was here in these cliffs," I whispered as we peeked out from behind the statue. "But you wouldn't believe me. Even when I told you I could feel chills—"

"Ra, that's it." Khepri turned to me. "That's the solution!"

What did he mean? I was too sick with fear to ask. Pharaoh's Cat is as brave as a lion, but even a lion is afraid of the gods. Anubis was striding up to the sarcophagus, his power so strong that flames leaped from the walls as he passed. Or maybe it was just that his flaming torch was reflected in every spark of gold.

Certainly, there was a lot of gold here. Gold on the statues. Gold on the table. Gold on the wall paintings. Gold from the stolen loot of Setnakht's tomb.

My paws trembled as Anubis set his torch in a golden stand, then leaned over the giant stone sarcophagus. With a horrible scrape, he pried the lid open and muttered some magic spell.

As I watched in horror, the mummy inside moaned and began to rise.

My ears flattened in fear, but I still caught every sound. The mummy groaned again, a tortured spirit being dragged back from the realm of the dead. The wrappings fluttered, releasing a terrible stench, like something that had rotted away . . .

I couldn't take it anymore. Shutting my

eyes, I went limp. *Please don't let Anubis find me.*

"I don't believe it," Khepri breathed into my ear. "Look, Ra. It's Kenamon."

Kenamon? Impossible!

I opened my eyes. The mummy was squirming now, and his face was turned toward us. Khepri was right. It really *was* Kenamon—tightly bound and gagged with torn linen wrappings.

Anubis hauled the boy out of the sarcophagus and dumped him on the floor. Grunting, the god straightened, and his jackal head wobbled. He steadied it with both hands.

It was a mask!

My claws sprang out. Nobody fools Ra the Mighty and gets away with it. Whoever it was, I was going to bring him to justice—somehow.

The boy groaned.

"It's your own fault," the man in the Anubis mask told him. "You should have kept your nose where it belonged, boy. No one asked you to snoop around."

So Kenamon had been trying to solve the case—just like us.

I peered at the jackal-head mask. Who was behind it? Was it the Scribe, or Huya, or Neferhotep? They were all about the right size, and the mask muffled the man's voice, so I couldn't tell.

"I was only taking what was rightfully mine," the man said to Kenamon. "All those years I've worked myself to the bone to give the pharaohs a blissful eternity, and what do I have to show for it? I've been shorted on pay and treated like dirt."

Shorted on pay? That didn't sound like the Scribe. That must mean it was Huya or Neferhotep.

"So who could blame me?" the man went on. "I can't right the balance in this life, but I can in the next. With the treasures I've taken, I'll have a glorious afterlife."

Not if you're a thief, I thought. *The real Anubis will weigh your heart, and you'll be found wanting.*

But the man in the mask didn't see it that way. "The gods themselves want me to have it," he told Kenamon. "Why else would they have led me to this ancient tomb when I was digging my own? Why else would I

have had the skills to disguise the passageway between them?"

*The skills to disguise the passageway
between them?* I thought of the woodwork
in Huya's tomb. If only we could have taken
a closer look at it!

"The gods planned it all," the man went
on. "They showed my ancestors the secret
way between Thutmose the Second's
tomb and Setnakht's. When Thutmose the
Second's tomb was robbed and abandoned,
I knew it was a sign. The gods ordained
that I should restore the balance. And then
you"—he pointed an accusing finger at
Kenamon—"went and stood in the gods'
way."

Kenamon tried to roll over.

"Squirm all you like," said the man. "You
won't get away from me. Nobody knows
where you are. I talked to the Scribe, and
even to those fools Huya and Neferhotep,
who have been combing the hills for you.
None of them suspect a thing."

What? If this man wasn't the Scribe or
Huya or Neferhotep, then who could he be?
The Vizier? The Captain of the Guard?

I exchanged a baffled glance with Miu, but Khepri didn't move a smidge on my head. So he wasn't startled by this revelation.

I gulped and thought hard.

That's the solution, Khepri had said. But what had we been talking about?

I'd been saying that no one would listen to me about Anubis, that they'd made fun of the chills I'd felt . . .

What was the connection? As I tried to figure it out, the man in the Anubis mask yanked the boy off the floor.

"When they find your body in the desert sands, with a tiny earring in your hand, everyone will know that you and your father are guilty. And they will never, ever come after me."

His hands went to the boy's throat, and I looked at Miu in panic. We had to stop him! And then, as I saw the golden cat sarcophagus behind Miu, it was as if I heard Pamiu speaking to me. I knew what to do.

Maybe Miu heard him, too, because when I darted out, she was right behind me.

"*Meeeeeeeow!*" I screeched.

The man let go of Kenamon. "What's that?"

I dashed over to the loot and grabbed a jewel in my mouth. Miu followed suit.

"Go, go, go!" Khepri shouted, clinging to the top of my head.

"Stop!" The thief abandoned Kenamon and chased after us. "Put that down!"

Miu and I raced ahead, the thief close behind us both. When we came to the pit, Miu soared over it, but I stopped in my tracks. A snarling shadow was leaping over the pit in the other direction, coming straight toward me.

Miu dropped her jewel and called out, startled, "Sabu?"

The thief tried to slow down, but we were too much of an obstacle. As I swerved to avoid Sabu, the man stumbled over me and lost his balance.

"No!" Sabu leaped to save him. Tail and feet tangled.

The man and the cat went hurtling into the pit, screeching and screaming.

CHAPTER 25

In the Pit

"Sabu?" Miu called down into the deep pit. "Cousin?"

"Don't waste your sympathy, Miu," Khepri said. "They're both guilty."

"What do you mean?" she said. "Sabu is on our side . . ."

I was just as confused. Taking care not to fall over the edge, we peered into the pit. In the deep shadows, you could just see them both: Bek breathing but unconscious next to the cracked Anubis mask, and Sabu licking his face.

"Sabu, don't!" Miu cried. "He's a thief and a kidnapper."

Sabu looked up and snarled at her. "And he almost got away with it, too—

until you poked your nose in."

"You mean, you knew he was guilty?" Miu said uncertainly.

"Of course I knew," Sabu bragged. "We're a team. I helped him. I was there in the tomb with him, and I put together an alibi—"

"You *lied*?" Miu said.

"—and I got that goose to back me up," Sabu went on.

"How?" I wanted to know.

"Blackmail," Sabu said, preening over his cleverness. "I told her I'd keep her goslings safe—no cat would touch them—but only if she did what I told her to do."

That explained why the goose had threatened to report me to Sabu.

"And that wasn't all," Sabu went on. "When Lord Fancypaws and his beetle started asking too many questions, I'm the one who pushed the brick onto them." His green eyes glittered balefully at me. "Too bad I missed, but it shut you up for a while. Just not long enough. That's why I had to plant that earring in Pentu's paint box."

Miu's ears flicked in disbelief. "And here I thought you were our partner."

"Partner to Lord Fancypaws?" Sabu sneered. "Never. I was hoping the jackals would finish you off. I told them they'd find a good meal at the tombs tonight—"

"You told the jackals where we were going?" I was floored.

Sabu laughed. "Sure. They're old friends of mine, and they'd do almost anything to please Bek. They love the meat he feeds them."

"So that's how Bek got the jackals on his side," Khepri murmured to me. "I bet it's why we found bits of spiced goose in the tomb."

Miu let out a plaintive meow. "Sabu, that's practically murder."

"I'd do it again if I could," Sabu said coolly. "Not just for Bek's sake, but for my own." Far below us, his tiger face twisted. "Why should Lord Fancypaws get a perfect afterlife, when I don't? That golden sarcophagus should be *mine*."

He spat at us, and Miu gazed down at him in dismay.

"Ignore him," I said to her. "We need to look after Kenamon."

Miu crossed over to our side of the pit and joined us at the boy's side.

"You're limping," Khepri said to her.

"I twisted my paw," she said, "but it'll be okay. I'm more worried about Kenamon."

I was, too. The boy's eyes were barely open.

"His breathing doesn't sound good," Miu said. "Maybe that gag is choking him."

"Let's chew through the ropes and free him," I suggested.

As Sabu yowled and swore at us from the bottom of the pit, we worked in turns.

When I took over from Miu, she tucked herself by Kenamon's shoulder. "I never thought a cousin of mine would do something so terrible."

"He had us fooled, too," Khepri said. "At least for a while—until Ra found the vital clue."

"And what was that, Ra?" Miu asked.

Thankfully I was chewing the rope, so I just pointed my tail to Khepri. Let him answer that.

"When Ra felt the 'breath of Anubis' in Bek's tomb, he was sitting near the secret entrance to this much grander tomb," Khepri explained. "The chill he felt was the air from the ancient tomb flowing out. That was the first clue that it was Bek."

"Goodness." Miu blinked. "How clever of you to figure that out."

"Um-hmmmmmmmph," I said, gnawing at the rope.

"Well, you had other things on your mind," Khepri said to Miu. "You were trying to save us from the jackals."

"I thought we'd ruled Bek out," Miu said. "He wasn't a suspect because he wasn't part of the crew that cleaned out the abandoned tomb."

"That was our mistake," Khepri admitted. "We didn't consider that there might be another way to work out how to get into Setnakht's tomb. But when we first came here, we heard that Bek's father and forefathers had been sculptors in the Valley of the Kings, working on all the pharaohs' tombs. That means they would have worked on Thutmose the Second's tomb when it was first made, and on Setnakht's tomb, too. And since they were sculptors, working with stone, they were more likely than most to notice a loose block—or to engineer one."

The rope that held the gag was starting to give way.

"My guess is that they passed the secret on, from son to son," Khepri said. "Maybe it was a joke at first, or simply an observation. But with Bek, it became the start of a plan. He thought the gods were calling to him. And Sabu agreed with him when he saw that cat sarcophagus."

I bit down hard on the rope. Poor Pamiu! He hadn't stood a chance.

Khepri waved his foreleg at the golden case, still glowing in the fading light of the torch. "That was the other clue. Most thieves would have melted the sarcophagus down, or shoved it in with the rest of the treasure. Instead it was set carefully aside, as if it was being saved for a one-of-a-kind cat. That sounded like Sabu to me. After all, he's the leader of the cats in Set Ma'at. So I started thinking about all the obstacles and dangers we'd faced in solving the case, and I realized that Sabu could have been behind them all."

As Miu shook her head sadly, I nipped at the last strands of rope that held the gag tight. "There!"

The rope snapped, and Kenamon spat out the gag. As soon as he croaked out his thanks to us, his eyes shut and his head slumped back on the floor.

Miu brushed her tail over his face, but that didn't revive him. "Oh, dear."

"We have to get him out of here. But how?" Khepri sounded as worried as I felt.

Miu pulled her tail back. "We need some humans to help us."

"And that means getting past the jackals," I pointed out.

There was a long silence.

Miu couldn't go, not with her sore paw. Khepri wouldn't get there till next week. So that left me. But after the worst day of my life—and the scariest night—was I up to facing the jackals again?

Pharaoh's Cat would volunteer. Pharaoh's Cat was braver than brave. But I didn't feel much like Pharaoh's Cat anymore. Once all the fancy trappings were gone, maybe all that was left was a not-very-brave cat.

Kenamon opened his eyes and struggled to smile at me.

Then again, maybe I was braver than I thought. What was it Miu had said earlier? *What matters is how we treat others in this life. That's the true memorial.* Much as I hankered after a marvelous tomb, I suspected she was right.

I brushed against Kenamon's cheek. His face pale with effort, he breathed, "Ra . . . the . . . Mighty."

Well, that settled it. The boy needed me. Me, Pharaoh's Cat. Even if I felt like a not-very-brave cat on the inside.

I rose. "I'll go to Set Ma'at now."

"And the jackals?" Miu said, eyes wide with concern.

I was already headed out. "If they try to stop me, they'll be sorry."

CHAPTER 26

Follow the Cat

I only realized that Khepri was with me when I made it to the other side of the pit, headed down the tunnel that led outside.

I stopped. "This is a dangerous job. You don't have to come with me."

"Oh, yes, I do," Khepri said calmly. "Miu's going to look after Kenamon, and I'm going to look after you."

He was smaller than my paw, and he was going to look after me? Ridiculous, of course, but I couldn't shake him.

"I'm sticking with you," he kept saying, and since I couldn't pry him off my ear, we continued down the tunnel together.

Truth to tell, I was glad he was there with me, especially when we slipped from the tunnel into Bek's tomb. (Just as Khepri had predicted, there were some loose blocks by the ledge where I'd felt the "breath of Anubis." Bek had pushed them back so that he could crawl through.)

"Do you see any jackals?" I asked as we peered out of the tomb.

"I only see stars," Khepri said. "Wow, they sure are bright out here in the desert."

"They are." Then I looked down to the east and saw Set Ma'at aglow with tiny lights.

"See that?" I said to Khepri. "They're awake, even though it's the middle of the night. Something's going on."

"Maybe they're searching for Kenamon," Khepri suggested.

"Probably for the wrong reason," I said.

"It's a good thing they've got us to set them straight." Khepri settled himself more firmly between my ears. "Let's go, Ra!"

Ears and eyes on the alert for jackals, I clambered down the cliffs. When we reached the bottom and no jackals had appeared, I felt more confident. I picked up the pace as I crossed the desert sands. Ahead of us, Set Ma'at shone brightly.

"So what's the plan?" Khepri asked.

"It's simple. I get someone to follow me back to the tomb."

"Who?" Khepri wanted to know.

"The Scribe, maybe—"

"But he thinks you're a stray," Khepri pointed out. "He'll just shoo you away."

Hmmm . . . I hadn't thought this part through. But Khepri was probably worrying over nothing. He often does that.

"It will work out," I said. "If need be, I'll tackle the Vizier when he comes to get me. He'll be here first thing in the morning."

"What if he isn't?" Khepri said.

"He won't have a choice. Pharaoh must have figured things out by now, and he'll be furious with the Vizier for bringing back an imposter."

"Unless Pharaoh thinks the imposter is you," Khepri said.

"He wouldn't," I said. "You said so yourself, Khepri. There's no cat like me."

"Well, I know that, and you know that.

But the humans are more easily fooled than we are—"

"Not Pharaoh," I insisted. "We have a special bond. He'll send the Vizier for me. And the Vizier will be in big trouble for mistreating me, so he'll have to do what I want. I'll lead him to the boy."

"If you say so," Khepri said doubtfully.

He didn't argue after that. But he didn't have to. As I padded through the dark toward the walls of Set Ma'at, tiny doubts pricked at me. What if Khepri was right? What if Pharaoh had accepted the imposter? I'd seen enough to know that, for many humans, all cats were alike. Maybe Pharaoh, at heart, thought one cat was as good as another. Maybe the special bond between us wasn't really so special after all . . .

"Ra?" Khepri clutched at my ear. "There's someone on our trail."

"*Anoooooooooooooooooooobis!*"

The howl came from close behind us. I bounded forward as fast as my paws would take me.

"Jackals!" On the top of my head, Khepri was rotating and shrieking. "Two of them. No, three . . . four . . ."

"Counting doesn't help!" I yowled.

I thought I'd been running fast. Now I discovered I could go faster. But so could the jackals. As I streaked toward the village gates, their baying came closer and closer.

"Ra, the gates are closed!" Khepri yelled in my ear.

"Then I'll climb straight up the wall!" My shriek echoed across the sands, so loud everyone in the village must have heard it.

I heard a familiar shout. Or was it just that my senses were failing me? I had never run so fast in my life, and my whole body was pounding from the effort.

The village gates began to open, ever so slightly.

Could it be? I wondered.

"Faster, Ra!" Khepri begged.

I didn't think faster was possible, but then a jackal nipped at my tail.

"*Anoooooooooooooooooooobis!*"

I yowled and darted through the tiny gap in the gates. They slammed behind me, locking the jackals out. With Khepri holding tight, I ran to the man with the familiar shout . . .

"Oh, Ra!" Pharaoh raised me in his arms. "Praise the gods, you're safe."

As a crowd gathered, I heard Khepri's stunned voice in my ear. "Pharaoh recognized you, Ra. Even without your collar, and with the mud and grit in your fur, he *recognized* you."

"Of course he did." I aimed for a lofty, confident tone, but I was too relieved to sound anything but delighted. "I told you: Pharaoh and I have a special bond. I never doubted it." *Well, not really.*

Pharaoh stroked my cheeks and fed me chunks of spiced ibex from his very own hand. "Forgive me, Ra. I was so busy yesterday that I didn't realize till midnight that the Vizier brought back the wrong cat."

"O Ruler of Rulers." The Vizier's voice

floated up from the ground, where he was lying flat by Pharaoh's feet. "I abase myself."

Cradling me in his arms, Pharaoh took a step away.

"I'll bet he won't be Vizier for very long," Khepri whispered to me.

"Let's hope not." I gulped down another morsel of ibex.

"I came to Set Ma'at to search for you myself," Pharaoh told me. "I turned the whole village upside down—and then I heard you out in the desert." He hoisted me up, so that we were eye-to-eye. "What on earth were you doing out there?"

I almost choked on my ibex. In the excitement of the moment, I'd nearly forgotten about Kenamon. I leaped from Pharaoh's arms and ran to the gate.

"Catch him!" the Scribe cried, and the crowd began to chase after me.

"Stop!" At the sound of Pharaoh's deep voice, everyone froze. "Let him be."

Pharaoh strode up to me. "What is it, Ra? It must be something important, if you're willing to brave the jackals again." He stared

down at me, his dark eyes thoughtful, and
then gave orders to his guards:

"Open the gates. Bring your torches. And
follow that cat!"

CHAPTER 27

I Can Explain

What was the best part of that night?

If you guessed the spiced ibex, you would be wrong. Not that it wasn't delicious. But the best part came later, after we reached the tomb.

Pharaoh followed me in, his guards close behind, trailed by the Scribe and the Vizier. They were startled to discover Bek and Sabu in the pit with the Anubis mask, and they gasped when they saw the stolen loot. But Pharaoh looked most shaken when he saw Kenamon.

"The boy trapped me!" Bek shouted from the pit. "He's the real thief."

"And Pharaoh's Cat helped him," Sabu yowled.

Ignoring this, Pharaoh ordered the guards to untie Kenamon. His breathing eased once he was freed from the tight wrappings, and after he drank medicine the guards gave him, he was strong enough to talk. At first, he was so overawed by Pharaoh that he could hardly find the words to say what had happened. But then Miu and I climbed onto his lap and purred, and soon the story poured out of him.

He had indeed seen the meat in Setnakht's tomb, and the loose block, but he had been afraid to tell anyone.

"Why were you afraid?" Pharaoh's voice was as gentle as it was with his own children.

"I was afraid they would call me a trouble-maker, and that Father and I would lose our jobs," Kenamon explained. "The Scribe calls Father a troublemaker because he's complained about the cuts in our wages. He even threatened to dismiss him. When the Vizier came, Father hoped he would set matters right, but he didn't. He got angry with Father, too."

Pharaoh's impressive eyebrows lowered in a frown. "There have been cuts in wages?"

The Scribe had been over in a corner having a quiet word with the Vizier, but now he bustled forward. "O Ruler of Rulers, the dear boy has misunderstood the situation—"

Pharaoh silenced the Scribe with a look.

Kenamon glanced nervously at the Scribe.

"You are under my protection," Pharaoh told Kenamon. "Answer freely. Your wages were cut?"

Kenamon nodded. "Last year they were cut for almost everyone in the village, and again during flood season."

"Not by me," Pharaoh said grimly.

"I can explain," the Scribe babbled.

The Vizier looked panicked. "So can I."

"Hold them both for questioning," Pharaoh commanded his guards.

"Well, that explains why Pentu told Kenamon that things were going to get better, and why his little sister hoped they'd be rich enough to get a cat," Khepri murmured in my ear. "Pentu thought speaking to the Vizier would help. He didn't know it would only make things worse."

Pharaoh spoke gently to Kenamon again.

"So how did you come to be here?"

"I couldn't stop thinking about what I saw in Setnakht's tomb," Kenamon said. "I told Father about it, but he was afraid that if we went to the Scribe, it would mean trouble for our family. He told me I should stay quiet. If I had seen the clues, surely others would, too. And if they didn't, perhaps I had just imagined them.

"I knew I *hadn't* imagined them," the boy went on, "but I didn't want to cause trouble for our family. So I thought I would try to track down the robber myself. If I could find the missing treasure, then no one could blame me, and my family might even get a reward."

I couldn't help feeling a certain amount of pride. The boy had all the traits of a Great Detective in the making. Well, except for being human, of course. But that was hardly his fault.

Kenamon's voice grew stronger, almost as if he could sense my approval. "I thought it might be Neferhotep who was the thief because he was acting like a rich man, buying lots of art for his tomb. But then

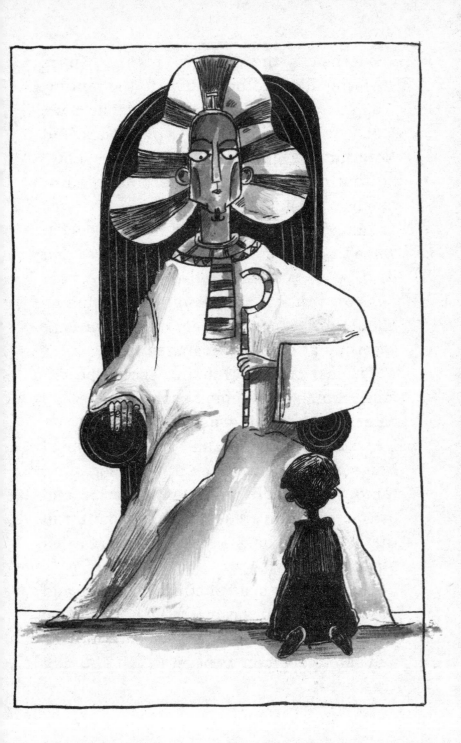

I overheard the Captain of the Guard scolding his brother Huya for gambling. 'You're acting all big and bold,' he said, 'and you're saying you'll win it back. But Neferhotep's got half your savings now.' So that explained why Neferhotep had so much to spend."

"Aha!" Khepri whispered into my ear. "It wasn't *gold* or *cold* that Boo overheard, but *bold*."

"No wonder Neferhotep was singing about how lucky he was, and Huya kept scowling at him,'" I whispered back.

"Then I started thinking about the village tombs," Kenamon continued, "and what a good hiding place they would be. I had a look around, and in Bek's tomb I found a secret entrance into another, older tomb. I was there when Bek came up and hit me." He shivered. "When I woke up in that sarcophagus, I thought I'd been buried alive."

I nudged my head against his hands and purred—my own way of urging him to go on with his story. Curving his arms around me and Miu, Kenamon went on to tell Pharaoh everything that had happened after that, including the way that Miu and Khepri and I had saved the day.

When he finished, Pharaoh said, "And then Ra the Mighty led me to you."

He and the boy both beamed down at me.

It was a wonderful moment. Even better than spiced ibex. But better still was the moment, an hour later, when we got back to Set Ma'at, and Pentu the painter was freed.

"Father!" Kenamon broke into a limping run. "It's me!"

"Kenamon." Pentu's wrists were chafed from the ropes, but he wrapped his arms tight around the boy.

"Now, that's what I call a happy ending," Miu said with satisfaction.

"And another mystery solved," Khepri said.

I didn't say anything, but I was pretty pleased. Yet again, Pharaoh's Cat was a hero.

Only one thing bothered me. I scratched at my scruffy coat.

"What does a cat have to do to get groomed around here?" I asked.

CHAPTER 28

Holding Court

Who knew they had such nice brushes, baths, and perfumes in Set Ma'at? Not that I'm a big fan of baths normally, but there's a time and a place for everything, especially if I'm being fed snacks. We went through the Scribe's most expensive toiletries, and I made quite a mess in his bathing area, but two hours later, as sunlight poured over Set Ma'at, I was back to my old self again.

"Wow, Ra." Khepri climbed back onto my head. "You are squeaky clean."

"Watch the feet," I said sternly. "Is that dung I smell?"

"The very best dung," Khepri reassured me with a happy sigh. "I went to Menwi's for breakfast."

I sat up, horrified. "Khepri! I've just bathed."

"Don't worry," Khepri said. "I wiped my feet. Er . . . and the rest of me."

"I should have made them pour on an extra bottle of perfume," I moaned.

"You smell fine," Miu told me. "More like a rose garden than a cat, to be honest, but—"

"As long as I don't smell like dung." I stretched out on the Scribe's steps to take in the sun. "Hey, do you see those cats over there, across the street? I think they're staring at me."

Miu checked them out. "The one on the left is your double, Ra. It must be the imposter."

I rolled over and squinted. "Impossible! You could hardly call him good-looking, could you?"

"No, but he does resemble you," Khepri said. "I wonder if he's hoping to take your place again."

I flexed my claws. "Just let him try."

"I don't think that's what he's saying." Miu tilted her head. "Listen."

I swiveled my ears and caught a few words.

". . . and then they put perfume on me, would you believe it?" the cat was saying to his friend. "It smelled even worse than those disgusting sauces they kept feeding me. I tell you, I've never been so glad to get back home. This is the good life here in Set Ma'at, no doubt about it . . ."

"You have got to be kidding me," I said as Miu and Khepri giggled.

"Tastes differ," Miu said.

"They certainly do." But that was just as well. I stretched back out on the step, content. "To each his own."

"Is Pharaoh still holding court in the Scribe's house?" Khepri asked Miu.

"He must be nearly done," Miu said. "While Ra was getting his bath, I went to listen. The Scribe and the Vizier had already confessed. They've been keeping back some of the workers' wages for themselves and blaming Pharaoh for the cuts. They accused each other of being the ringleader."

"But why didn't they investigate the

tomb robbery properly?" I asked. "They weren't involved."

"No, but each one thought the other was up to something, and they were hoping for a share of the profits."

"I bet they also worried that a full investigation would involve Pharaoh," Khepri said. "And they didn't want Pharaoh taking a closer look at Set Ma'at."

"Pharaoh's dismissed them from their posts now," Miu said. "They're in disgrace. They have to pay the villagers back double what they owe, plus heavy fines to Pharaoh. Huya's been dismissed, too. He was helping the Scribe cheat the other villagers."

"What about Bek?" I wanted to know.

"The punishment for tomb robbing is death," Miu said, "but Bek broke down completely and pleaded for forgiveness. Pharaoh says he'll spare Bek's life because of his family's long service, but Bek will still pay for his crimes. Pharaoh is sending him to one of the royal quarries."

"So he'll spend the rest of his life under guard, chipping away at a rock face?" Khepri said. "Yikes!"

"He disturbed the eternal rest of a pharaoh and his cat," I reminded Khepri. "And he was going to kill Kenamon."

"Yes, he was willing to sacrifice the boy just so he could have a glorious afterlife." Miu sighed. "Honestly, why do people get so obsessed with their tombs?"

"Not just people." Khepri glanced at me.

"Hey," I said, stung. "I'm not obsessed."

They exchanged a look.

"Okay, maybe I am, a little," I admitted. "But I know when to step back. I'm not like Bek or Sabu."

"Speaking of which," Khepri said, "there they go now."

The guards were marching Bek down the street, arms tied behind his back. Seeing him pass by with his head bent low, it was hard to believe he'd been the mighty figure in the Anubis mask who had terrorized Kenamon.

Trailing behind Bek and the guards, Sabu wailed, "It's not fair!" When he passed us, he hissed and leaped for me. "I'll make you pay for this, Fancypaws!"

I jumped up to fight, but Pharaoh had

come to my side. Seeing him, Sabu slinked away and followed Bek out of the village.

Pharaoh looked down at me fondly. "A friend of yours, Ra?"

He's a very clever man, Pharaoh. But sometimes he completely misses the point.

Oh, well. He's still my Pharaoh. I curled my tail and sat in the perfect Bastet position at his feet.

"It's good to see you looking like yourself again," he told me. "Well, almost yourself."

Almost? I was taken aback. Had someone missed a spot in my grooming?

As I made a discreet inspection of my paws and rear, Pharaoh gestured to the doorway behind us, where Kenamon stood with his father. Aside from some grazes from the ropes, the boy looked strong and well. Even better, he looked happy.

As he came forward, Pharaoh put something sparkling in his hand. "Kenamon, perhaps you would put this on Ra?"

"With pleasure, Great Ruler of Rulers."

It was my collar! My own, golden collar. I stood proudly at attention while Kenamon fastened it.

"I'm going to give you the best tomb portrait any Pharaoh's Cat ever had," Kenamon whispered. When I nuzzled his fingers, he smiled. "Come back soon, Ra the Mighty."

I brushed my whiskers against his hand. *I will.*

"Time to go home, Ra," Pharaoh said.

In the midst of dusty Set Ma'at, our splendid litter shone like a small sun. As Pharaoh held back the shimmering curtains, I leaped up onto it. Khepri was on my head, with Miu close behind.

"Your reward shall be paid in gold," Pharaoh said to Kenamon. "And perhaps you will come to the palace one day, and paint these three together." He gestured to the pillows where Khepri, Miu, and I had settled down.

"O Ruler of Rulers, I would be honored," Kenamon said, beaming.

"Did you hear that, Miu?" Khepri hopped off my head and bounced on the pillow. "We're going to have our portrait painted, too."

"And we'll get to see the boy again." Miu sounded pleased.

As Pharaoh spoke with the boy and his father, Khepri said, "You know, Ra, we never did get to see your tomb."

"That's okay." I sprawled back on the

pillows. "If you ask me, tombs are over-rated."

Miu and Khepri looked startled.

"True," Miu said, "but I never thought I'd hear you say that, Ra."

"No, never," Khepri agreed.

"A cat can change his mind," I told them as Pharaoh climbed in beside us. "Especially Pharaoh's Cat. Life is for living, that's what I say."

"And for being Great Detectives," Khepri said eagerly.

"And making friends," Miu added, looking fondly at Khepri and me.

"That's right!" I dug into the bowls that Pharaoh offered us. "And don't forget the snacks."

Beneath us, the magnificent litter swayed, and we headed back to Thebes.

Ra's Glossary of Names

Anubis (ah-*noo*-bis): The jackal-headed guide of the afterlife—and maybe a hair-raising haunter of tombs.

Bastet (*bas*-tet): The most elegant goddess around. Naturally, she's a cat.

Bek (*bek*): A remarkable sculptor who loves his job—and his cat, Sabu.

Boo (*boo*): Surprisingly likable, considering he's a dog. Much too fond of games.

Huya (*hoo*-yah): A carpenter with a smirk, big biceps, and a very fierce goose. The Captain of the Guard's little brother.

Isesu (ee-*seh*-soo): Kenamon's little sister, who knows what she wants.

Kenamon (*ken*-ah-mon): Sharp-eyed boy genius and portrait painter. Gifted cat carrier.

Khepri (*kep*-ree): My scarab beetle buddy. A fan of mysteries and dung.

Menwi (*men*-wee): A corker of a porker, and the Scribe's favorite pet. A lady who needs her beauty sleep.

Miu (*mew*): Friend and fellow Great Detective. Champion of the underdog, even though she's a cat.

Neferhotep (nef-er-*hoe*-tep): A lucky goldsmith with itchy fingers and lots of rings.

Nefru (*nef*-ru): Neferhotep's kitten. What did she see—and how much does she know?

Pamiu (*pah*-mew): Former Pharaoh's Cat and beloved companion of Setnakht. Entered the afterlife in a snazzy gold sarcophagus.

Pentu (*pen*-too): Kenamon's father. Rabble-rouser, tomb painter, and worried dad.

Sabu (*sah*-boo): Miu's cousin and the feline boss of Set Ma'at. Definitely *not* a Great Detective.

 240

Set Ma'at (*set mah*-aht): "The Place of Truth"—that is, the village where the tomb workers live. (If you ask me, they should have called it "the Place of Dust.")

Setnakht (*set*-nahkt): Pharaoh's forefather. Illustrious companion of Pamiu. Owner of a magnificent tomb.

Thebes (*theebs*): A glamorous city with an elegant palace. Some of the best cat grooming in the kingdom takes place here.

Thutmose (thoot-*moh*-seh) **the Second**: One of Pharaoh's distant ancestors, whose afterlife went up in smoke.

Note

No one knows for certain how ancient Egyptian hiero-
glyphics were pronounced. Even Egyptologists don't
always agree on how to say them. A name as simple as
Thebes can be pronounced *"teebs"* or *"theebs"*—and there
are other possibilities, too.

Author's Note

When I close my eyes, I can still see the photos from the first article I ever read about "King Tut" (aka the pharaoh Tutankhamun). I was about nine years old, the same age Tutankhamun was when he became pharaoh. I was awed by the golden treasures in his tomb—and even more by the tale of how that tomb was robbed, resealed, and discovered again thousands of years later. I've been fascinated by ancient Egypt and its tombs ever since. It was a pleasure to write more about those tombs in this book, and especially to write about their creators, the people of Set Ma'at.

The village of Set Ma'at really did exist. As Ra explains, its name meant "the Place of Truth." Located on the West Bank of the Nile across from Thebes, it was the home of the workers who built the royal tombs in the Valley of the Kings (including the one for Tutankhamun). The village existed for roughly five hundred years, from about 1550 to 1080 BCE. Nowadays the site is called Deir el-Medina, and only the ruins remain, but those ruins are very important. From them, we've learned a lot about the lives of ordinary people in ancient Egypt.

We know, for instance, that the tomb workers lived very close together, in houses with several ground-floor rooms, a cellar, and a roof terrace. High officials like the Scribe of the Tomb lived in grander houses. Other top-ranked officials included the foremen, who oversaw teams of carpenters, stonemasons, sculptors, painters, and other artisans. (Often a foreman became the boss of Set Ma'at, instead of the Scribe.) For a long time, there was a high wall around the entire village.

Tomb workers often passed their jobs from father to son, and children could begin working in the tombs at a very young age. Tomb workers made a better living than most people in ancient Egypt, so a talented boy like Kenamon could expect to do well. There weren't enough jobs to go around, however. That's one reason why some people from Set Ma'at became tomb robbers.

Tomb workers could only enter the Valley of the Kings at specific times, in teams, and under guard. They were closely watched. Nevertheless, some workers managed to steal treasures from right under the guards' noses. Others joined gangs that broke into the tombs at night. There were also plenty of tomb robbers who had no connection to Set Ma'at at all.

To prevent break-ins, special guards patrolled the Valley of the Kings, keeping watch over the existing tombs and the tombs-in-progress. When royal finances were tight, fewer guards were hired, and tomb robberies became more frequent.

Pharaohs who were short on money also cut tomb workers' wages. When payments didn't show up on time, the workers sometimes went on strike. Usually the pharaoh and his advisors found the funds to pay them. Otherwise there would be no tomb—and that would mean a terrible afterlife for the pharaoh.

Ancient Egypt did not have coins or currency as we know them today. Instead, the tomb workers were paid in bread and beer and other goods. Bonuses could be paid in oil, salt, and meat. Set Ma'at also received many basic supplies from the government for free, including housing, water, vegetables, fish, firewood, pottery, and even clothing.

Workers also bargained (and sometimes gambled) with one another, not just for everyday items, but also for goods they could use in the afterlife. Their tombs were set into the cliffs near the village, just as this book describes, and they were much simpler than those of the pharaohs. If you ever go to Deir el-Medina, you can visit some of them.

Making these private tombs took up a lot of the workers' spare time. But they had rich family lives, too. Children's toys have been found in the ruins of Set Ma'at, and we know that villagers enjoyed games, parties, feasts, and festivals. They also kept pets, and they were fond of cats. Lively drawings of cats appear on a number of Set Ma'at ostraca (broken pieces of pottery with writing on them). It's fun to imagine Kenamon making a sketch like that of Ra.

Believe it or not, there really were cat mummies in ancient Egypt. The most valuable were put into a cat-shaped mummy case, or sarcophagus. Many thousands of cat mummies have been found at Bubastis, a city that was dedicated to the worship of the cat goddess Bastet. One ancient account says that cats from all over Egypt were buried there. Sadly, many scholars think most of these cat mummies come from sacrifices at Bastet's temple. Yet some cat mummies—especially the ones in beautiful cases—were probably much-loved pets, and their owners must have hoped to see them again in the afterlife.

The name of Boo, the guard dog, is a tribute to Abutiu (sometimes spelled Abuwtiyuw or Abwtjw), a real Egyptian dog who lived over four thousand years ago. He was a royal guard dog who served a Sixth Dynasty pharaoh. We don't know who this pharaoh was, but he loved Abutiu so much that he ordered his masons to build a special tomb to honor him.

In ancient Egypt, the animal most associated with tombs (and with the god Anubis) was the jackal. According to recent DNA evidence, a more accurate name for the Egyptian jackal would be the African golden wolf. The name jackal has a long history, however. Outside of scientific circles, people are likely to stick with it, as I've done here.

Setnakht and Thutmose II were real pharaohs who were buried in the Valley of the Kings. Setnakht's mummy was moved around and eventually disappeared. For the purposes of this story, I have relocated his tomb. Thutmose

II's mummy was discovered in 1881 in a cache of more than fifty royal mummies. No one is certain where his original tomb was—but it may yet be found. In fact, if you become an archaeologist, you may be the one to find it!

That's one of the most marvelous things about ancient Egypt. There are so many mysteries waiting to be solved.

A Note About Sources

There are entire libraries of books about ancient Egypt, and especially about its tombs. The books that were most helpful to me in writing this story were:

Morris Bierbrier, *The Tomb-builders of the Pharaohs.* Cairo: The American University in Cairo Press, 1989.

Anton Gill, *Ancient Egyptians: The Kingdom of the Pharaohs Brought to Life.* London: HarperCollins, 2003.

Jaromir Malek, *The Cat in Ancient Egypt.* London: British Museum Press, 1993.

Nicholas Reeves and Richard H. Wilkinson, *The Complete Valley of the Kings: Tombs and Treasures of Egypt's Greatest Pharaohs.* London: Thames & Hudson, 1996.

Ian Shaw and Paul Nicholson, *British Museum Dictionary of Ancient Egypt.* London: British Museum Press, 1995.

Acknowledgments

Ra and I are very lucky indeed to have Sarah Horne bringing his adventures to life again with her amazing art. Thank you, Sarah!

My warmest thanks also go to Sara Crowe and the entire Pippin team, and to the terrific people at Holiday House, especially Mora Couch, Emily Campisano, Emily Mannon, Terry Borzumato-Greenberg, Mary Cash, Kevin Jones, and my brilliant editor, Sally Morgridge. I'm indebted to copyeditor Barbara Perris, too.

I'm also grateful to Paula Harrison and Kit Sturtevant for their insightful comments on an early draft, and to Paula (again!) and Mo O'Hara for supporting Ra's debut. I treasure the friends and family who have encouraged me, especially Karl Galle and Sylvia Atalla, who brought me my writing mascots all the way from Cairo. My thanks also go the Ashmolean Museum and the British Museum, whose Egyptian galleries never fail to delight, move, and inspire me.

I would be lost without my husband and daughter, who raced through early drafts, laughed in all the right places, and remain Ra's biggest fans. Thank you, my sweethearts! I wouldn't trade you for anything, not even a golden, cat-shaped sarcophagus.